HER NAME WAS KALIN
AND SHE WAS A WITCH. . .

She came running down the long road, long legs flashing beneath the hem of a golden tunic. It was cut away from her arms, her throat, falling to mid-thigh and cinctured with a crimson belt. Flame red hair was bound with a fillet of gold. Her face was deathly pale, the eyes enormous, the red lips parted as she fought for breath.

Behind her seethed a yammering, screaming mob.

"They'll get her," breathed the seller of symbiotes. He looked pale, sick. "They'll run her down for sure."

He broke off as she tripped and fell, naked flesh white against the gold, white and gold stark against the flame-bright cobbles of the street. "Earl!" he yelled. "Earl, you crazy fool! Come back here!"

Dumarest paid no attention. He ran, face hard as he estimated time and distance. He could reach the girl before the mob. It was a thing he had to try.

She looked up at him, eyes pools of green fire in the translucent pallor of her face. Her hands lifted, white butterflies of defense. "No!" she said. "No!"

"Witch!" shrieked a voice. "Don't let her get away!"

KALIN

E. C. TUBB

SF
ace books
A Division of Charter Communications Inc.
A GROSSET & DUNLAP COMPANY
51 Madison Avenue
New York, New York 10010

KALIN
Copyright © 1969 by E.C. Tubb

Dedicated to John Edwin

An ACE Book

This Ace printing: July 1982
Published Simultaneously in Canada

2 4 6 8 0 9 7 5 3 1
Manufactured in the United States of America

I

IT WAS BLOODTIME on Logis and the captain was
firm. "I am sorry," he said, "but I will take no
chances. As passengers you are free to go or stay
as you desire, but I must tell you this: if the perime-
ter fence should be penetrated I will seal the ship.
And," he added significantly, "it will remain
sealed until all danger is safely past."

"You would leave us outside?" The woman
wore clothes too young for her raddled features,
her cracked and aging voice. "Leave us to be
killed?"

"If necessary, madam, yes."

"Incredible!" Gem-fire flashed from her hands
as they moved in the cone of light streaming from
above the open lock. "To treat your passengers
so!"

Her companion, a scarred mercenary, growled deep in his throat. "The captain has no choice, my dear. His first duty must be for his ship." He looked at the officer. "Am I not right?"

"You are a man of understanding, sir," said the captain. "As you say, I would have no choice. Bloodtime on Logis is not a gentle period. Usually the field suffers no depredation, but beyond the fence anything can happen." His eyes, flat, dull, indifferent, glanced from one to the other. "Those who venture into town do so at their own risk. I would advise you all to restrain your curiosity."

A thin-faced vendor of symbiotes stared thoughtfully after the retreating figure. "He's exaggerating," he said. "Inflating the potential danger in order to keep us all nicely to heel."

"Maybe he is, but he wasn't joking about sealing the vessel." A plump trader fingered the charm hanging about his neck, a good luck symbol from one of the Magic worlds. He looked shrewdly at Dumarest. "You've traveled, Earl. You've seen a lot of the galaxy. What do you advise?"

Dumarest looked at the trader. "About what?"

"You heard what the captain said. Do you think he was exaggerating? Would it be safe for us to go and see the fun?"

Dumarest made no comment. From the vantage point at the head of the ramp on which they stood he had a good view of the city. It sprawled, an ill-lit shapeless conglomeration of buildings beyond the high wire mesh of the fence. It was barely night but already the red glow of fire painted the lowering clouds. The soft breeze carried the echoes of screams, shouts, the savage baying of a mob.

The woman shivered. "Horrible! Like animals. Dogs worrying a bone. Why?" she demanded. "Why in a so-called civilized community do they do it?"

Her companion shrugged. "It is their custom."

"Custom!" She wasn't satisfied. Her eyes met those of Dumarest, held with dawning interest. "A word which explains nothing. Why do they throw aside all law, all restraint?"

"To cleanse themselves, my lady," said Dumarest. "At least, that is what they claim. Once, perhaps, the thing had purpose but now it has become a vicious habit. For three days the population of Logis will hunt and kill, hide and die." He looked at the flames. "Burn and be burned."

But not all of them. Only the weak and helpless, those without friends willing to lend their protection. The old days when harmful mutations, the insane, the crippled, the physically weak and morally vicious were culled from society were over. Now old scores would be settled, debts and grudges paid, revenge taken. A few politicians would be hunted down for their lying promises. Some cheating traders, businessmen, company heads would be sacrificed to appease the mob. But, when it was all over, those in power would still remain.

The woman shivered again at the echo of a scream. Her hand glittered as she touched the arm of her companion. "Let's go inside," she said.

"We can sit and talk and play cards, maybe. Listen to music, even. Anything but this. I have no love for the sounds of violence."

And, thought Dumarest watching, neither had the man. Not now. The mercenary was old and afraid of what the future could bring. A man who had too often seen the amniotic tanks, suffered the pain of wounds. Now he searched for a haven and the woman could provide it. She too had lived a hard life but, unlike the man, she had something to show for it. Jewels instead of scars. Together they could find comfort if not happiness.

Dumarest turned, breathing deep of the night air, suddenly conscious of his isolation and a little envious of those who did not travel alone. Behind him the trader shuffled, restless, his eyes reflecting the glow of mounting fires.

"Let's go down to the gate and take a closer look," he suggested. "That should be safe enough. We could take care and might see something interesting."

"We might," agreed the thin-faced vendor. He sucked in his cheeks. "It seems a pity to come all this way and see nothing. It won't happen again for another year and who knows where I'll be then?" He nodded, deciding. "All right. I'll come with you. How about you, Earl?"

Dumarest hesitated and then, slowly, followed the others down the ramp.

Guards stood by the gate, armed, armored and sullen. They were field personnel selected to remain stable during the three day period. They were carrying weapons which were rare on Logis—automatic rifles. These could fire a spray of shot as effective if not as lethal as lasers at short range. One of them glared as the three men approached.

"You going out or staying in?"

"Staying in," said the trader promptly. He squinted past the guards into the town. A wide road, apparently deserted, ran directly from the gate. "How bad is it?"

"Not bad at all," said the man. His face was hard, brutal beneath his helmet. "Those who asked for it are getting it." His face convulsed in sudden rage. "Damn it! I shouldn't be here at this lousy gate. I should be out there hunting down the bastard who stole my wife!"

"Take it easy," said one of his companions. He wore the insignia of an officer. "That's no way to talk. You got divorced, didn't you?"

"What's that got to do with it?"

"She got married again, didn't she?"

"So?"

"Forget it," said the officer. "I'm not looking for a quarrel. But you volunteered for gate-duty. You swore that you had no grudges to settle and that you could use the extra pay. So you're here and you're going to stay here for the duration. Get it?"

"Go to hell!"

"This is your last chance, Brad."

"—you!"

The officer reached out and snatched the rifle from the guard's hands. "All right," he said coldly. "That's enough. Now beat it."

"What?" The man blinked. "Now wait a minute!" he stormed. "I've got a right to—"

"You're relieved," snapped the officer. "I don't want you on this gate. Now get to hell out of here while you've still got the chance."

Dumarest looked at the officer as the man walked away mouthing threats. "He'll get you for this."

"No he won't," said the officer. "Brad's a coward and a bully and that's a poor survival combination. He's made too many enemies and won't last until dawn." He sucked thoughtfully at his teeth. "A little insurance wouldn't hurt though," he mused. "I know his ex-wife. She's a decent woman married to a trained fighter. I'll tip them off about what has happened. Just in case," he explained. "Some rats have a lot of luck and Brad might just about make it to their apartment."

"But that's as far as he'll get," said Dumarest.

"Sure," agreed the officer. "That's the whole idea." He walked to where a booth stood beside the gate, to a phone and his warning call.

Dumarest joined his companions where they stood looking down the road. There was little to see. Fires sent drifts of smoke billowing across the street. The sound of breaking glass came from the business section where shops which had economized on shutters were providing meat for the looters. A band of men appeared, lurched toward the gate and then disappeared into a tavern. Light shone from the open door but quickly vanished as the panel slammed. The trader licked his lips.

"A drink," he said. "I could do with something to wet the gullet." He licked his lips again. "How about it, Earl? Shall we walk down to that tavern and order a bottle? Hell," he added, "why not? No one can possibly have cause to hate us on this planet, so where's the danger?"

It was there: Dumarest could smell it, sense it riding like smoke on the air. The blood-craze of normally decent people suddenly relieved of all restraint. More. Proving themselves by being the first to accuse, the loudest to complain, the quickest to act.

Among such people, how long would a stranger last?

The thin-faced vendor moved restlessly. He was getting cold and bored and thought longingly of the comfort waiting in the ship. Also he should attend to his samples. That symbiote from Een: it was time he wore it. If he put it off too long the thing would encyst to sporofulate which, if not tragic, would be an inconvenient nuisance.

A shout came from down the road. A man lurched from between two buildings, a bottle in one hand, a long knife in the other. He crossed the street, stood swaying, then vanished down an alley. Another followed him, a woman with long, unkempt hair. She carried a crude club made of a stone lashed to a stick. Crude, but effective enough if swung against a skull. On Logis revenge wasn't forestalled by poverty.

"She's after him," said the trader. "Did you see that, Earl? She's tracking him down as if he were a beast. Waiting until she can sneak up on him and smash in his head.'' He chuckled. ''Unless he sees her first.'' he qualified. ''He wasn't carrying that knife for fun.''

''Murderers,'' said the vendor. He sounded disgusted. ''Let's get back to the ship and breathe some clean air.''

The trader bristled. ''Now wait a minute—''

''Murderers,'' repeated the vendor. ''Not you, them. I enjoy a little excitement as much as the next man but what are we seeing? An even match? A regulated bout with ten-inch knives, first-blood winner or to the death? An even melee? Listen,'' he emphasized. ''I've got a couple of symbiotes in the ship which will give you all you could hope for. You ever seen leucocytes chase malignant bacteria? With one of my pets you can really join in. Mental affinity achieved on a sensory plane and, what's more, the thing takes care of you while you feed it. Really takes care.'' He winked. ''Guess what I mean?''

''I can imagine.'' The trader hesitated. ''These symbiotes come expensive, right?''

The vendor nodded. ''Tell you what,'' he suggested. ''I'll rent you one. I've got a thing from Een which would suit you right down to the ground.'' He read the other's expression. ''You're wondering if they're safe. Would I be selling them if they weren't? They're symbiotes, man, not parasites. They give you something in return for what they take. Look,'' he urged. ''Ask anyone. The captain, the medic, anyone. They'll tell you the same.''

''All right,'' said the trader. ''I'm convinced.

Let's get back to the ship.'' He looked at Dumarest. ''Coming, Earl?''

Dumarest didn't answer. He was staring down the wide street. A flicker of gold showed in the distance. It vanished, reappeared with a sudden burst of resplendency, vanished again as a leaping flame died. It shone again with reflected brilliance, coming nearer, closer, with the sound of racing feet. Beside him the trader sucked in his breath.

''By God,'' he whispered. ''It's a girl!''

She came running down the road, long legs flashing beneath the hem of a golden tunic. It was cut away from her arms, her throat, falling to mid-thigh and cinctured with a crimson belt. Flame red hair was bound with a fillet of gold. Sandals of gold hugged her feet showing the scarlet of painted nails. Her face was deathly pale, the eyes enormous, the red lips parted as she fought for breath.

Behind her seethed a yammering, screaming mob.

''They'll get her,'' breathed the seller of symbiotes. He looked pale, sick. ''They'll run her down for sure.''

''Run her down and tear her apart,'' agreed the trader. He narrowed his eyes. ''She's trying to reach the gate,'' he murmured. ''With luck she might make it. Not that it'll do her any good but—'' He broke off as she tripped and fell, naked flesh white against the gold, white and gold stark against the flame-bright cobbles of the street. ''She's down!'' he groaned. ''They'll get her now for sure.'' He sensed movement, the shifting of the guards, the stir of displaced air. ''Earl!'' he yelled.

"Earl, you crazy fool! Come back here!"

Dumarest paid no attention. He ran, face hard as he estimated time and distance. He could reach the girl before the mob. He might just be able to reach her and return to the gate before they covered the distance. It was a thing he had to try.

She looked up at him, eyes pools of green fire in the translucent pallor of her face. Her hands lifted, white butterflies of defense. "No!" she said. "No!"

His words were quick, harsh. "I mean you no harm. Can you stand? Run?"

She moved, winced. "My ankle—"

There was no time for more. He stooped, gripped her wrist and hauled upward. The impact of her body was light on his shoulder. He felt the smoothness of her naked thigh against the palm of his left hand, the warmth of her body against his cheek. He ran toward the gate, seeing the faces of the assembled guards, their lifted weapons, the watchful eyes of his two companions.

"Earl!" called the trader. "Behind you!"

Something struck his leg. Something else clawed at his arm. He spun, lashing out with his free hand, saw a snarling face fall away. A man, quicker than the rest, had reached him and had tried to tear the girl from his shoulder. Dumarest set her on her feet and thrust her toward the gate.

"Move!" he ordered. "Hop if you have to, but move!"

"But you—"

"Damn it, girl, don't argue!"

He turned just in time to avoid an ax swinging at

his skull. He stepped backward, caught the haft, tore it free and slammed the side of the blade into the wielder's mouth. He fell, spitting teeth and blood, screaming as feet trod him to the stone. A knife flashed in the firelight. Dumarest lifted an arm and blocked the blade. It slashed his tunic; the edge sliced through plastic and grated on the metal weave below. He struck out with the ax, felt it stick, released the haft as a thumb gouged at his eyes. He kicked and felt bone snap beneath his boot. With both hands stiffened he moved slowly back toward the gate: chopping, stabbing with his fingers, kicking, using elbows and head as a weapon. Lashing out, always on the move, always on the attack.

Abruptly he was standing alone, ringed by savage faces, the moans and whimpers of the injured rising above the soft rustle of advancing flames, the ragged sounds of breathing.

A man spat a mouthful of blood. "Listen," he said. "I don't know who you are but we want that girl. Do we have to kill you to get her?"

"You could try," said Dumarest.

"We can do more than that," said the man. "You're one against the lot of us. You're quick and you're fast but how long do you think you can hold out?"

"Be sensible," urged someone from the rear of the crowd. "What's the girl to you? Hell, man, why lose your life trying to protect someone you don't even know?"

"You've done enough," said a third. "Maybe you don't understand, so we'll let it go. But try to stop us again and you'll get taken apart."

Dumarest edged a little further from the ring of faces. They were talking, normally a good sign: men who talk rarely act. But these people were degenerate rabble taking advantage of the Blood-time to slake their lust for violence. They were talking to summon up their courage, not to arrive at a compromise.

Dumarest glanced over his shoulder. The girl stood before the assembled guards, her eyes wide as she watched the mob. Why didn't she pass through the gate into the field?

The first speaker wiped blood from his mouth. "She can't escape," he said. "The guards won't let her through the gate. Only those with booked passage are permitted on the field at Bloodtime. There's no sanctuary in there."

Dumarest raised his voice and called to the trader. "Seegihm."

"Earl?"

"Get a message to the captain. Have him book a passage for the girl at my expense. Use the phone and pass her through when it's done."

A woman screamed from the rear of the mob. "Mister, you're crazy! You don't know what you're doing. That girl's a witch!"

"That's right!" roared a man. "A dirty, filthy, stinking witch! She hexed my daughter so that she aborted!"

Others took up the chorus. "She called up a wind to rip the roof off my barn!"

"I had a whole brewing ruined through her!"

"My boy lost an eye!"

"She dug a hole and my wife fell in it and broke a leg!"

"I bought stock and went broke. She did it!"

The shouts became an animal snarl.

"She did it! She did it! Witch! Stinking, lousy witch! Kill her! Burn her! Flay her alive! Kill! Kill! Kill!"

Dumarest retreated as they began to advance, then heard the frenzied shout of the trader.

"Back, Earl! Back! It's all fixed!"

He turned and dived for the gate, seeing the girl pass through with a flash of red and gold and gleaming white. The guards closed in behind him, presenting a solid front to the screaming mob, their hands tight on their weapons, their eyes oddly red.

"Witch!" shrieked a voice. "Don't let her get away!"

The mob howled, indifferent to personal danger, hurling themselves against the guards, their guns, the fence, smashing it beneath the pressure of their bodies, racing across the field to where Dumarest and the others ran up the ramp and into the open lock seconds before the captain sealed the ship.

II

HER NAME WAS KALIN and she really was a witch.

She sat facing Dumarest at the table in the lounge of the ship, watching as he shuffled a deck of cards. They were alone. Seegihm, the trader, lay in his bunk, a purple symbiote wreathing his neck, his eyes closed in a sleepless dream. The vendor was busy with his stock. The woman and her companion stayed in her cabin. The crew, as always, took care not to mingle with the passengers.

"Now," said Dumarest. He cut the deck into three stacks. "You know this game?"

She nodded. "Highest, lowest, man-in-between. You want me to pick the winning card?"

"If you can."

"This one," she said after a moment's thought. The tip of one slender finger rested on the left-hand stack.

Dumarest turned over the cards. The others

showed a ten and a three; hers a seven. As man-in-between she would have won the pot. Again he shuffled, taking special care not to see the cards, taking even more care that the pips were shielded from her view. Again she chose the winning stack. And again, again—ten times in all before he called a halt.

Thoughtfully he leaned back and looked at the girl. She had bathed and the terror and strain had left her face and eyes. They were still green pools of fire, still enormous in the translucent whiteness of her face, but now she looked what she was, an amazingly attractive woman instead of a hunted animal.

"Kalin," he said. "Kalin what?"

She shrugged. "Just Kalin."

"No Family? No House? No Guild?"

"There are people who live without such things," she said. "You, for example."

"You know?"

"I guessed," she admitted. "But it's pretty obvious. You have the look of a man who has learned to rely on no one but himself. A man who has lived hard and alone. The way you saved me shows that. Other men would have waited for someone to tell them what to do. You simply acted. If you had hesitated I would have been killed."

"Hunted down for being a witch," he said. "Are you?"

"Am I what? A witch?"

He waited, watching.

"I don't know," she confessed. "Just what is a witch supposed to be? I told people things," she explained. "I wanted to be friendly and tried to warn them: a woman who ate bread made of diseased grain, a boy who was chopping wood and lost an eye, about a substance in which a woman fell. I warned them," she said bleakly. "But they took no notice and then, when they had hurt themselves, they blamed me."

"Naturally," he said. "They would hardly blame themselves for ignoring your advice." He paused, and then abruptly asked: "What were you doing on Logis?"

"I was born—"

"No," he interrupted. "You were never born on that planet. Not with your color skin and hair. And why try to lie to me? What's the point?"

"None," she admitted, "but sometimes a lie can save a lot of explanation." She lifted her head, met his eyes. "I was born a long way from here on a planet close to the Rim. Since then I've traveled a lot. I joined up with a necromancer who took me to Logis. We worked there: telling fortunes, reading palms, astrology, all that stuff. I think he had a sideline in chemical analogues. I know for sure that he dealt in abortifacts and hallucinogens. He tried to sell me a few times but I wouldn't be sold." Her eyes were clear, direct. "You understand?"

Dumarest nodded. "And?"

"I slipped a knife into him at Bloodtime. That made it legal. They couldn't touch me for doing that. The rest you know."

"Tell me."

She bit her lower lip, teeth white against the bloom of redness. "They came for me. The ones I'd tried to help. They were like animals. If I hadn't moved fast they would have torn me to pieces." She reached out and touched the sleeve of his tunic. "You saved my life," she said. "I'm not going to forget that."

He felt the warmth of her nearness, caught the scent of her hair, the biological magic of her body. Her eyes were green wells into which a man could immerse his being. The translucent skin reflected the light as if made of living pearl.

Deliberately he picked up the cards, shuffled and began to deal, the pasteboards vanishing from his hands to instantly reappear on the surface of the table. The magic of quick-time did that. Not accelerate the cards but slow his metabolism down so that he lived at one-fortieth the normal rate. He, the girl, the others who traveled on High passage. The drug was a convenient method to shorten the apparent time of the journey, to shrink the tedious hours.

He leaned back, looking at the lounge, seeing the duplicate of a hundred others he had known on as many similar ships. Soft padding, a table, chairs, an overhead light. The inevitable furnishings of a small ship catering to few passengers.

"That one." Her finger touched a stack of cards. Unconsciously he had dealt for highest, lowest, man-in-between. He turned it over. Again she had picked the winner.

He rose, crossed to the spigots, drew two cups of Basic, handed one to the girl as he returned. Sitting, he sipped the thick, warm liquid. It was sickly with glucose, heavy with protein, laced with vitamins; a cupful contained enough nourishment to supply a spaceman's basic needs for a day. A heating element in the base of the container kept the liquid warm during its long journey from wall to table, from table to mouth.

Dumarest put down his empty cup and looked at the girl. "The people of Logis were right," he said. "You are a witch."

Her eyes clouded. "You too?"

He shrugged. "What else can you call someone who can see the future?"

"A freak," she said bitterly, and then, "How did you know?"

Dumarest reached out and touched the cards. "You won too often. It couldn't have been telepathy because I took care not to see the pips. You couldn't have cheated because you didn't touch the cards. Teleportation would serve no purpose unless you knew which stack to move where. And it couldn't have been simple luck, not with such a high score. So," he ended quietly, "there can only be one explanation."

Kalin was a clairvoyant.

The mirror was made of a lustrous plastic, optically perfect, yet cunningly designed to flatter the user when seen in a special light. Sara Maretta had no time for such deceit. Irritably she snapped on the truglow tube and examined her face. Old, she thought, and getting older. Too old and stamped with time and experience for ordinary cosmetics to be of much use, no matter how thickly applied. A complete face transplant was what she needed.

The fair skin and smooth contours of a young girl to replace the sagging flesh and withered skin. A complete face-transplant and more. The breasts and buttocks, the thighs and calves, the arms and hands. Especially the hands.

I need a new body, she thought looking at them. A complete new body and, if rumor were true, she might get one. The surgeons of Pane, so it was whispered, had finally solved the secret of a brain transplant. For money, a lot of money, they would take out her brain and seal it within the skull of a young and nubile girl. It was a rumor, nothing more, yet a rumor she desperately wanted to believe.

To be young again! To watch the fire kindle in a man's eyes as he looked at her. To thrill to the touch of his hands. To live!

Looking at her, Elmo Rasch read her thoughts as if her mind had been an open book. The mercenary leaned against the wall of the cabin, eyes hooded beneath his brows, mouth a thin, cruel line. Deliberately he reached out and snapped off the truglow tube. With the dying of the harsh light she lost ten years of apparent age.

"Elmo?"

"Why hurt yourself?" he said quietly. "Why twist the knife for no purpose. Is it so necessary to be young again?"

"For me, yes."

"Was youth such a happy time?" His voice held bitterness. "If so you were luckier than I. But perhaps you enjoyed the Houses where you were paraded for sale. The mansions of depravity."

She looked at him and smiled without humor. "Where men like you," she said softly, "lined up to pay for pleasure you would not otherwise obtain."

"True." He dropped to sit beside her on the bunk, his thigh hard against her own. Reflected in the mirror his face was a mass of crags and hollows, the thin line of scar tissue a web-like tracery. "Soon," he said. "Very soon now."

He saw the faint tremble of her hands. On her fingers the gems flashed in living rainbows. Elmo reached out, touched them with a blunt finger.

"Pretty, aren't they?" he said mockingly. "Good enough to delude, but you and I and any jeweler know what they are really worth. Stained crystal with plated settings. The cost of a short High passage, perhaps, certainly no more."

"Are your scars worth as much?"

"Less," he admitted. "Which is why we are together. Why we must work as a team. My experience and knowledge; your money. What you had of it. And," he said meaningfully, "you have very little left."

And that was as true as the rest of it. A lifetime of work to end in what? Degradation and poverty. Of what use was a woman when she was ugly and old? Sara looked at her companion. Elmo left much to be desired but he, at least, understood. And yet, woman-like, she wished that he had been other than what he was.

A man like Dumarest, for example. She could trust a man like that. Trust him to drive a hard bargain, perhaps, but to keep it to the bitter end.

Had she been younger he would not be traveling alone. Even now she could dream, but long ago she had learned to live within her limitations. She could love Dumarest but he would never love her. And now, with that girl from Logis—

Irritably she shook her head. Dreams, stupid dreams at a time like this!

Elmo reached into his pocket and produced a flat case. He opened it and the light winked from polished metal and unbreakable glass. The hypo-gun was a work of art, a multi-chambered model calibrated to a hair. It would air-blast any one of a half-dozen drugs in a measured dose through clothing, skin and directly into the bloodstream.

"I could only afford one," he said. "But it's loaded and ready to go."

"Are you sure?" She was practical. "Are the drugs as specified? You could have been cheated," she pointed out. "Transients are easy prey."

Elmo growled deep in his throat. A mannerism to add emphasis. "The last man who tried to cheat me lost an eye. The drugs are good. I checked them before handing over the money. Your money," he said flatly. "But, Sara, never was cash more wisely spent."

Gem-fire betrayed her agitation.

"A few minutes," he said. "That's all it will take. A brief flurry of action and our troubles are over. The ship and all it contains will be ours. Ours, Sara! Ours!"

His eyes glowed and she wished that she could share his supreme confidence. And yet the plan made sense. To attack the crew, drug them into insensibility, take over the vessel was, basically, simple enough. Piracy, as a crime, was not unknown, but to take over a vessel was not enough. The thing was to dispose of it. Spacemen were clannish and united against all who threatened their security. Even the cargo of a stolen ship would be almost impossible to sell.

And yet Elmo claimed to have solved the problem.

It was possible he had, but his vagueness at times irritated her to the point of rebellion. Then he would remind her of what wealth could bring, but never could she forget the penalty of failure.

"You know what will happen if they catch us," she said. "Eviction into space with a suit and ten hours' air. Doped so that a scratch will feel like the slash of a knife. Our senses sharpened so that we'll scream our throats raw." Her hands clenched as she thought about it, the brown spots on their backs standing ugly against the skin. "Elmo! If they should catch us!"

"We'll die," he said. "A little before our time, perhaps, but we'll die and that is all. A few years lost against what? But we won't fail," he insisted. "I've been over this a thousand times. First the steward and his hypogun. It'll be loaded with quick-time. You take it and use it on the lower deck crew. I'll tackle the officers, a shot of serpenhydrate and they will be marionettes, helpless to do other than obey. They will alter course, take the ship where we want it to go, land it as it needs to be landed."

"And then?" She liked this part, liked to hear

him say it again and again as though, by repetition, hope could be turned into fact.

"Money," he said thickly. "Enough to buy the new body you desire. Enough for me to hire an army and win a principality, a planet, an empire! The galaxy, Sara! Ours for the taking!"

Simple, she thought. So very simple. Too simple. Surely, somewhere, there must be a catch?

Then she caught sight of her face in the mirror and longing overwhelmed her doubts.

It was like the spread fingers of a hand. Five pictures, sometimes more, but only five were of any real use. The others were too vague, too hopelessly indistinct.

"The strongest one is the future," Kalin explained. "I concentrate and there it is. Like cards," she said. "I wanted to win so I looked to see which pack would win and chose that one."

And because she chose it, it won; because it won, she chose it. A closed cycle to ensure that the visualized future would be correct.

"The other pictures?" asked Dumarest. "Are they alternates?"

She frowned. "I think so. Like the cards again. Two showed different packs which lost. Two, very vague, showed no cards at all."

Alternate universes, thought Dumarest. Or rather alternate futures in which they had not played cards or had stopped playing them. Unless?

"The time element," he said. "Can you determine it? Can you select how far you will see into the future? An hour, a day, a year?"

She shook her head, frowning. "No, not with any great accuracy. Some things are big and stand out even though the details are vague. Others, smaller and closer, are very clear. I could see the cards without trouble. "I can see other things," she said. "One of them is very strong. You are kissing me," she told him. "That and something else." Her hand reached out for his own. "We are going to become lovers," she said quietly. "I know it."

"*Know* it?"

"It is there," she insisted. "When I concentrate about us and look into the future it is there and it is very sharp and very strong." Her eyes searched his face. "Earl! Is something wrong?"

He shook his head.

"Is the prospect so distasteful?"

He looked at her and felt her attraction. The biochemical magic of her flesh transmitted through sight and sound and smell. She was beautiful! Beautiful!

Beautiful and the possessor of a wild and wanton talent which caused men to call her witch!

She moved and a trick of the light turned her hair into a cascade of shimmering silver, painted elfin contours on her face. *Derai!*

Dumarest felt his nails dig into his palms, the sweat bead his forehead.

"Earl!" She moved and the illusion was broken. Once again the hair was billowing flame, the face a rounded pearl. "Earl, what is it?"

"Nothing. You reminded me of someone, that is all."

Jealousy darkened her eyes. "A woman?"

"Yes." He opened his hands and stared at the idents on his palms. "Someone I once knew very well. Someone who—" He took a deep breath. "Never mind. She's been gone a long time now."

"Dead?"

"You would call it that."

He leaned back, again calm, able to stare at her with detachment. A clairvoyant. Someone who could see into the future. There were others with similar talents and some with even more bizarre; among the scattered races of mankind mutation and inbreeding had done their work, but all had one thing in common. All seemed to have paid a physical price for their mental abilities.

What was wrong with Kalin?

Mentally he shrugged; time alone would tell. In the meanwhile he could speculate on her talent. It must be like a man at sea sailing through objects misted with uncertainty. In the distance, looming gigantic though unclear, the mountain of death could be seen across a lifetime. Closer, the hills of age, misfortune, birth, illness, disaster—visible for years. Then the things which could be determined for perhaps months. Smaller events unclear beyond a day. Trifles which had a visible range of minutes or even seconds.

To Kalin her talent was merely an extension of her vision.

He felt the warmth of her hand resting on his

own, the strength of her fingers as she squeezed. "Earl," she said. "Come back to me."

"I'm here."

"You were thinking," she said. "Of what? Places you have seen? People and planets you have known?" The fingers tightened even more. "Where is your home, Earl? Which planet do you call your own?"

"Earth."

He waited for the inevitable derision but, to his surprise, it didn't come. He felt a momentary hope. The girl claimed to have traveled. It was barely possible that she might—

"Earth," she repeated, and shook her head. "An odd name. Dirt, soil, loam, but you don't mean that, of course. Is there really a planet with such a name?"

"There is."

"Odd," she said again, frowning. "I seem to have heard of it somewhere, a long time ago. When I was a child."

A child?

Age was relative. For those traveling Low time it had no meaning. For those traveling High, using the magic of quicktime, an apparent year was two generations. But no matter how time was judged, the girl could not be older than twenty or twenty-five biological years.

Less when the real standard was used. The only measure that had true meaning. Experience.

"Try to remember," he urged. "What you know about Earth."

She smiled. "I'll try. Is it important?"

Was a reason for living important? Dumarest thought of all the journeys he had made, the ships he had ridden, sometimes traveling High, more often traveling Low. Doped, frozen and ninety percent dead, riding in the caskets meant for the transport of animals, risking the fifteen percent death rate for the sake of economy. Traveling, always traveling, always looking for Earth. For the planet which seemed to have become forgotten. The world no one knew.

Home!

He waited, watching her as she closed her eyes, frowning in concentration, doing what came hard to her—looking back instead of forward, fighting her natural inclination.

Was the price she paid for her talent the inability to recall the past?

She opened her eyes and saw the impatience registered on his face, the hope. "I'm sorry, Earl."

"You can't remember?"

"No. It was a long time ago. But I'm sure that I've heard the name somewhere. On a tape or in a book, perhaps. Earth." She repeated it softly to herself. "Earth."

"Or Terra."

She raised her eyebrows.

"Another name for Earth," he explained. So much, at least, had he learned. "Does it strike a chord?"

"I'm sorry, Earl, I wish that it did but—" She

shrugged. "If I were back home I could have the library searched, the records. If it was there I would find it."

"Home," he said. "Where is that?"

"Where my love is," she said and then, "Forgive me, Earl, I didn't mean to joke. But you look so solemn." She narrowed her eyes as if just thinking of something. "Earl, if you come from this planet Earth, then surely you must know the way back. Can't you simply go back the way you came?"

Dumarest shook his head. "It isn't as simple as that. I left when I was a boy: young, scared, alone. Earth is a bleak place scarred by ancient wars, but ships arrive and leave. I stowed away on one. The captain was old and kinder than I deserved. He should have evicted me but he allowed me to live." He paused. "I was ten years old. I have been traveling ever since: moving deeper and deeper into the inhabited worlds, into the very heart of the galaxy, becoming, somehow, completely lost." He smiled into her eyes. "You find it strange?"

"No," she said. "Not strange at all. Home," she mused. "The word holds a magic that is unique."

"And your home?" His voice was soft, gentle—picking up the trail of her thought so that she responded automatically, without thinking, without restraint.

"Solis."

"Solis," he repeated, "where the library is, the

clue to Earth you mentioned.'' He reached out and pinched a tress of hair between finger and thumb. ''I think,'' he said gently, ''that I had better take you home.''

III

BROTHER JEROME, High Monk of the Church of Universal Brotherhood, tucked thin hands within the capacious sleeves of his robe and prepared to enjoy his single hour of daily recreation. As usual he chose to walk alone, sandals noiseless on the smooth plastic of floors, ramps and stairs. Again, as usual, he varied his route: taking in a little more of the vast building which, like the Church, was under his direct control and authority. A monk skilled in topography had worked out that, if Brother Jerome maintained the area covered by his daily perambulations, it would take well over a year for him to fully inspect the entire building.

Today he chose to walk beside some of the chambers of indoctrination, conscious in his sedate pacing of the quiet hum of ceaseless activity. It was a comforting sound and one he liked to hear. It reassured him that the Church was thriving and strong and growing as it must: expanding so as to carry the message to people everywhere that the

Universal teaching of complete Brotherhood held
the answer to all pain, all hurt, all despair. No man
is an island. All belong to the *corpus humanite*.
The pain of one is the pain of all. And if all men
could be taught to recognize the truth of the
credo—*there, but for the grace of God, go I*—the
millennium would have arrived.

He would never see it. Men bred too fast,
traveled too far for any monk now alive to see the
fruition of his work. But it was something for
which to live, a purpose for their dedication. If a
single person had been given ease of mind and
comfort of spirit, then no monk had lived and
worked in vain. The strength of the Church rested
on the importance of the individual.

He paused beside the door, shamelessly listening to the voice from within the chamber. Brother
Armitage was giving a group of novitiates the ini-
tial address. They had passed the twin barriers of
intelligence and physical ability; now he assailed
their minds.

". . . this. Why do you wish to become monks?
That question must be answered with frankness,
honesty and humility. Is it in order to help your
fellow man? No other answer can be accepted. If
you hope for personal reward, for gratitude, power
or influence, you should not be here. A monk can
expect none of these things. If you seek hardship,
privation, the spectacle of pain and anguish, then
the Church does not want you. These things you
will find, but they are not things to be sought. Man
is not born to suffer. There is no intrinsic virtue in
pain."

True, thought Brother Jerome, grimly, Armitage was a good teacher: hard; tough; ruthless when it came to weeding out the unsuitables, the masochists, romantics, would-be martyrs and saints. Later he would show the class his scars and deformities, tell them in detail how the injuries had been inflicted and how, incredibly, he had managed to survive. Some would leave then. Others would follow, most after the hypnotic session in which they suffered a subjective month of degrading hardship. Simulated, naturally, but terrifyingly effective. Those remaining would progress to be taught useful skills, medicine, the arts of hypnosis and psychology, the danger of pride and, above all, the virtue of humility.

One class among many, all working continuously, all doing their best to meet the constant demand for Hope-trained monks. There were other schools on a host of planets, but always those trained in the heart and center of the Church were in greatest demand. They carried the pure teaching, they had been taught the most modern methods and techniques; what they knew they could pass on.

Like a continuous stream of healing antibiotics, thought Brother Jerome. The metaphor pleased him. An endless series of ripples, he thought, spreading, cleansing, widening to impinge on every planet known to mankind. A great flood of love and tolerance and understanding which would finally wash away the contamination of the beast.

There was tension in the office. Brother Jerome sensed it as soon as he returned and he halted in the outer room, letting his eyes take in the scene. The wide desk with its normal office machinery. The waiting space with the seats for those who had appointments. The monks who acted as office staff and others—young, hard-bodied men born on high-gravity worlds, trained in physical skills and always found where there was need of care and protection. Brother Fran, of course, his personal secretary, and a man who stood with his back to a wall.

Curiously the High Monk looked at him, guessing that he must be the cause and center of the tension. He was tall, wearing a transparent helmet and a full, high-collared cloak which covered him from shoulder to heel. The fabric was of a peculiar golden bronze color and glinted as if made of metal. Above the high collar the face was scarred, aquiline; the nose a thrusting beak between smoldering, deeply set eyes. He glanced at Brother Jerome as he entered the room, then looked away as if he'd seen nothing of interest.

Fran came forward, his face calm above the cowl of his robe. "Brother," he said without preamble. "This man insists on seeing you. He has no appointment."

"I insist on seeing the High Monk," grated the stranger. "I will stand here until I do."

Brother Jerome smiled, appreciating the jest though it was obvious his secretary did not. He took two steps and faced the stranger. "Your name?"

"Centon Frenchi. I live on Sard."

"Is not that one of the vendetta worlds?"

"It is."

Jerome nodded, understanding. "If you wish you may discard your cloak," he said gently. "Such defensive clothing is unnecessary on Hope. Here men do not seek to kill each other for the sake of imagined insult."

"Be careful, monk," warned Centon harshly. "You go too far."

"I think not," said Brother Jerome evenly. He glanced to where two of the watchful attendants had stepped forward, and shook his head. He would not, he knew, have need of a bodyguard. "What is the nature of your business on Hope?"

"I will tell that to the High Monk."

"And if he does not wish to listen?" Jerome met the smoldering eyes. "You are stubborn," he said. "And you are also unrealistic. Why should you be permitted to jump the line of those who have shown the courtesy to make an appointment? Who are you to dictate what shall and shall not be?"

"I am Centon Frenchi of Sard!"

"Others too have names and titles," said Jerome smoothly. "Can you not give me one good reason why you should be given preference?"

Centon glowered at the waiting monk. He glanced around the office, empty but for the watchful staff. "No one is waiting," he said. "How can I give preference over people who are not here?"

"This is not a day for interviews and audiences," explained Brother Fran from where he stood to one side. "The High Monk has many other duties and you are keeping him from them."

"Him?"

"You are speaking to Brother Jerome, the High Monk of the Universal Brotherhood."

Jerome saw the shock in the Sardian's eyes, the flicker of disbelief. It was a familiar reaction and went with love of pomp and insistence on privilege. His age and frailty they could accept, for it took time to mount the ladder of promotion. His sandals and rough, homespun robe, exactly the same as that worn by any other monk begging in the streets, were harder to swallow. The concept behind his lack of ornamentation was sometimes beyond their capacity to understand.

And yet, he thought wearily, it was so very simple. He was a man no better, and he hoped no worse, than any other monk of the Brotherhood. Why then should he set himself apart? And to wear costly garments and gems would be to make a mockery of that in which he believed. But how could a man like Centon Frenchi understand that? Realize that to any monk the cost of a jewel to wear on his finger was to rob others of food . . .? Such baubles came expensive when measured in the price of suffering and pain which would otherwise have been negated.

"I am waiting," he said patiently. "If you are unable to convince me, then I must ask you to leave. You can," he added, "make an appointment for a later time."

The watchful monks moved a little closer, tense and ready for action. Centon looked at them, stared at Jerome. Breath hissed through his nostrils as he inflated his lungs. "I have supported the Church," he said tightly. "At times I have been most generous."

"And now you want something in return," said Jerome. "It is a natural reaction. But what you want and what others are willing to give need not be the same. I suggest you make an appointment in the normal manner."

He turned, feeling deflated, empty. Pride, he thought bitterly. A man makes a prison in which to live and calls it his pride. Sometimes the prison is so strong that he can never break out. Again he heard the hiss of inhalation. Something caught at his garment.

"Brother!" Centon's voice was almost unrecognizable. "Help me, Brother! For the love of God, help me!"

Jerome turned, smiling, waving off the guarding monks. His hand fell to the one gripping his robe. Centon's hand: big, scarred, the knuckles white as he gripped the fabric. "Of course, brother!" said the High Monk. "Why else am I here?"

The inner office was a sanctuary in which Brother Jerome spent most of his waking hours. It was a comfortable place, a curious blend of the ultra-modern and near-primitive. Books lined the walls, old, moldering volumes together with spools of visual tape, recording crystals, impressed plastic and molecularly-strained liquids which, when stimulated, resolved themselves into mobile representations in full, three-dimensional color.

There were other things. Little things for the most part, for a monk has to carry what he possesses and weight and size are limiting factors. A fragment of stone, a shell, a plaited length of plastic wire. A piece of curiously carved wood, a weathered scrap of marble and, oddly, a knife made of pressure-flaked glass. Centon looked at it, then at the placid face of the monk seated behind his wide desk. "An unusual object," he said. "Did you make it?"

"On Gelde," admitted Jerome. "A primitive, backward planet only recently rediscovered. The natives had forgotten much of what they knew and had developed a metal-worshiping religion. They confiscated my surgical instruments. I made that knife as a general purpose scalpel and used it during my stay." He dismissed the knife with a gesture. "And now, brother," he said gently, "you asked for my help. Tell me your problem."

Centon approached the desk and stood before it, the reflected light gleaming from his protective cloak. "I need to find my daughter."

Jerome remained silent.

"She left home many years ago," said Centon. "Now I need to find her."

"And you think that we can help you?"

"If you cannot, then no one can!" Centon strode the floor in his agitation, his stride oddly heavy. "I belong to a noted family on Sard," he said abruptly, then immediately corrected himself.

"Belonged." His voice was bitter. "Can one man claim to constitute a family? We held wide estates, owned factories, farms, a fifth of the wealth of the planet was ours. And then my younger brother quarreled with the third son of the family of Borge. The quarrel was stupid, something over a girl, but there was a fight and the boy died." He paused. "The fight was unofficial," he said. "Need I tell you what that means?"

On the vendetta worlds it meant blood, murder, a wave of savage killing as family tore at family. "You could have admitted guilt," said the monk quietly. "Your younger brother would have paid the blood-price and ended the affair."

"With his death? With each Borge coming and striking their blow, abusing his body, killing him a dozen times over? You think I could have stood for *that!*" Again the floor quivered as Centon strode in agitation. "I tried," he said. "I offered reparation to the extent of one-third of our possessions. I offered myself as a surrogate in a death-duel. They wanted none of it. One of their number had died and they wanted revenge. Three weeks later they caught my younger brother. They tied his feet to a branch and lit a fire beneath his head. His wife found him that same evening. She must have gone a little mad because she took a flier and dropped fire on the Borge estates, destroying their crops and farms. They retaliated, of course, but by then we were ready." He paused, brooding. "That was five years ago," he said. "That is why I need my daughter."

"To fight and kill and perhaps to die in such a

cause?'' Brother Jerome shook his head. ''No.''

''You refuse to help me find her?''

''If she were in the next room I would refuse to tell you,'' said the monk sternly. ''We of the Church do not interfere in the social system of any world, but we do not have to approve of what we see. The vendetta may be good from the viewpoint that it cuts down great families before they can establish a totalitarian dictatorship but, for those concerned, the primitive savagery is both degrading and cruel.'' He paused, shaking his head, annoyed with himself. Anger, he thought, and condemnation. Who am I to judge and hate? Quietly he said, ''If my words offend you I apologize.''

''I take no offense, Brother.''

''You are gracious. But is it essential that you find your daughter? Do you need her to end the vendetta?''

Centon was curt. ''It is ended.''

''Then—?''

''The family must be rebuilt. I am the last of my name on Sard. The name of Borge is but a memory.''

Brother Jerome frowned. ''But is your daughter necessary for that? You could remarry, take extra wives. You could even adopt others to bear your name.''

''No!'' Centon's feet slammed the floor as he paced the room. ''It must be my seed,'' he said. ''My line that is perpetuated. The immortality of my ancestors must be assured. It would be useless for me to take extra wives. I cannot father a child under any circumstances. Aside from my daughter I am the last of my clan and I am useless!''

Standing, facing the desk, he swept open his long cloak. Metal shone in the light: smooth, rounded, seeming to fill the protective material. Brother Jerome stared at half a man.

The head was there, the shoulders, the arms and upper torso but, from just below the ribs, the flesh of the body merged into and was cupped by a metal sheath. Like an egg, thought the monk wildly. The human part of the man cradled in a metal cup fitted with metal legs. He took a grip on himself. Too often had he seen the effects of violence to be squeamish now. The cup, of course, contained the surrogate stomach and other essential organs. The legs would contain their own power source. In many ways the prosthetic fitments would be better than the fleshy parts they replaced but nothing could replace the vital glands. It was obvious that Centon could never father a child.

''We miscounted,'' he explained dully. ''I was to blame. I thought all the Borge were dead but I overlooked a girl. A child, barely fourteen, who had been off-planet when the vendetta had begun. She was clever and looked far older than her age. She gained employment as a maid to my nephew's wife. Mari was expecting a child, a son, and was two months from her time. We held a small dinner party to celebrate the coming birth—and the bitch took her chance!''

Brother Jerome pressed a button. A flap opened in his desk revealing a flask and glasses. He poured and handed a glass to his visitor. Centon swallowed the brandy at a gulp.

"Thank you, Brother." He touched his face and looked at the moisture on his finger. "I'm sorry, but each time I think about it—" His hands knotted into fists. "Why was I so stupid? How could I have been such a fool?"

"To regret the past is to destroy the present," said the High Monk evenly. "More brandy?"

Centon scooped up the replenished glass, drank, set it down empty. "The dinner party," he continued. "All of us around a table. All that were left of the Frenchi clan on Sard. Myself, Mari, her husband Kell, Leran who was eight and Jarl who was eleven. Five people left from almost a hundred. It had been a bitter five years."

Brother Jerome made no comment.

"The Borge bitch was waiting at table, in attendance in case Mari should need her aid. She dropped something, a napkin I think, and stooped beneath the table. The bomb had a short fuse. The fire spread and caught her as she was trying to escape. She stood there, burning, laughing despite her pain. I shall always remember that. Her laughing as my family died." Centon took a deep breath, shuddering. "They burned like candles. I too. The flame charred my legs, my loins, but I had risen and was leaning over the table pouring wine. The board saved me. Somehow I managed to reach the escape hatch. By the time help arrived the room was a furnace and I was more dead than alive."

He wiped a hand over his face, dried it on his sleeve. "Often, when in the amniotic tank and later when relearning to walk I wished that they had let me go with the others. Then some of the pain died a little and I began to live again. Live to hope and plan and dream of the future.

He stepped close to the edge of the desk and leaned forward, arms supporting his weight, hands resting flat on the wood. "Now you know why I need my daughter," he said. "*Need* her. I do not lie to you, monk. I pretend no great or sudden love. But, without the girl the family is ended."

"Not so," corrected Jerome quickly. "She could be married with children of her own. The line will continue."

"But not on Sard! Not on the world we have won with our blood and pain!" Centon straightened, controlled himself. "And she may not have children yet," he pointed out. "She may never have them. She may die or be killed or rendered sterile. I want to find her. I must find her," he insisted. "I will pay anything to the man who can tell me where she is. The man," he added slowly, "or the organization."

Jerome was sharp. "Are you trying to hire the services of the Church?"

"I am a rich man," said Centon obliquely. "But I come to you as a beggar. Help me, Brother. Ask your monks to look for my daughter. Please."

The monks who were on every habitable world. Eyes and ears and sources of information. In the slums and the palaces of those who ruled, the homes of the wealthy and the streets of the poor. Everywhere the message of tolerance needed to be sown, which was everywhere in the galaxy.

Thoughtfully the monk pursed his lips. "You

have a likeness of the girl? Some means by which to identify her?"

Centon plunged his hand into an inner pocket and laid a wafer of plastic on the desk. Brother Jerome looked at the flame red hair, the pale, translucent skin, the green eyes and generous mouth. A panel gave details as to height, weight, measurements, vocal and chemical idiosyncrasies.

"Her name is Mallini, Brother. You will help me to find her?"

"I promise nothing," said the High Monk. "But we shall do our best."

IV

ELMO RASCH CHECKED the time and spoke to the woman. "Now."

She hesitated, trembling on the brink of irreversible action, then stiffened as she summoned her resolve. The reward was too great to be dismissed. Against renewed youth, death was a thing without terror. She rose and stepped toward the door of the cabin. Without glancing at the man she stepped outside into the passage. The steward sat in an open cubicle facing the lounge, a book open on his lap. It was of a type designed to educate and entertain those who were illiterate. The steward was not uneducated but, among spacemen, certain volumes held a special attraction. He looked up as Sara approached, and touched a corner of the page. The moving illustration of naked women faded, the whispering voice died. Casually he closed the book.

"Could I help you, my lady?"

"I feel ill," she said. "Sick. Have you something to reestablish my metabolism?"

She watched the movement of his eyes as, unconsciously, he glanced to where he kept his hypogun. It would be a common model loaded with quick-time for the benefit of those traveling High but it would serve her purpose.

"It would not be wise to travel Middle, my lady," protested the steward. "The journey is long and there will be complications."

Too many complications. More food and not the easily prepared Basic. The need for entertainment, books, tapes, films perhaps. The need for constant attendance and she had the look of a real harridan. And, more important, the captain would be far from pleased. It was the steward's job to keep things simple. Complications would cost him an easy berth.

"Look, my lady," he suggested. "Why don't you—"

His voice died as her fingers closed around his throat in a grip learned from her third lover. Deliberately, she squeezed the carotids, cutting off the blood supply to the brain. A little would result in unconsciousness, too much in death. Unconscious men could wake, cause trouble. It was better to make certain he died.

The hypogun in her hand, she looked back at her victim. He sat slumped in his chair. Time was precious but little things were important. She opened his book and rested it on his lap.

Naked woman twined in sinuous embrace to the

accompaniment of a whispering drone of carnal titivation.

Elmo looked at her face and nodded his satisfaction. "You did it. Good. You have the hypogun?"

She lifted it, put it into his hand. He lifted his own and shot her in the throat.

She felt nothing, not even the blast of air forcing the drug it carried into her bloodstream, but abruptly things changed. The lights dulled a little, small sounds became deeper pitched, surroundings took on a less rigid permanency. The latter was psychological.

Elmo stood facing her, the hypogun in his hand, motionless.

Motionless and utterly at her mercy.

He had made a mistake in neutralizing the quick-time in her blood before speeding his own metabolism. She could kill him now. She could do anything she wanted. She could do—nothing.

He had insisted that she kill the steward to prove herself, to blood her hands. He had treated her first in order to show his trust or to point out her weakness. To kill him was now to double her fault.

Reaching out she took the hypogun from rigid fingers, maneuvering it with care to avoid broken bones and torn flesh. She aimed, triggered, watched as he jerked back to normal-time existence.

"Tough," he said, and shook his head as if to clear his senses. "I don't—" He broke off and concentrated on what had to be done. He ejected a vial from the steward's instrument and replaced it with one from his pocket. "Just to make sure." He handed Sara the hypogun. "Now get moving and inject everyone you meet with quick-time. As long as we stay normal we'll have the edge." He stood looking at her. "Well?"

"We'll be apart," she said. "Out of touch. What if something goes wrong?"

"Nothing can go wrong." He stole time to be patient despite the screaming need for haste. "We've been over this a dozen times. Now move!"

He watched as she vanished from the cabin and down the passage toward the lower region of the ship. The scars writhed on his face as he watched her go. He who had once commanded the lives and destinies of a hundred thousand men to now be dependent on one old woman. And yet her desperation made her the equal of any. He could have done far worse.

Turning, he ran from the cabin toward the upper regions of the ship where the officers guided the vessel through the tortuous rifts of space.

Dumarest opened his cabin door and looked at the girl standing outside. Her eyes were wide, anxious.

"Earl, something is wrong."

He stood back to let her enter. "Wrong with you? The ship?"

"The ship, I think; it isn't very clear. I was lying down thinking of us. I was looking ahead, trying to—" She shook her head. "Never mind what I was looking for, but things were all hazy and dim

almost as if there were no future at all. And that's
ridiculous, isn't it, Earl? We're going to be together for always, aren't we?''

''For a while at least,'' he said. ''All the way to
Solis if nothing else.''

''You promise that?'' She gripped his hand and
pressed, the knuckles gleaming white beneath the
pearl of her skin. ''You promise?''

He was startled by her intensity. ''Look
ahead,'' he suggested gently. ''You don't have to
take my word for anything. You are able to see the
future. Scan it and satisfy yourself.''

She swallowed, teeth hard against her lower lip.
''Earl, I don't want to. Suppose I saw something
bad. If I'm going to lose you I don't want to know
about it. Not for certain. That way I'll always be
able to hope. It isn't nice knowing just what is
going to happen, Earl. That's why I'd rather not
know.''

''But you looked,'' he pointed out. ''You tried.''

''I know, but I couldn't help myself. I wanted to
be sure but, at the same time, was frightened of
knowing the worst. Does that make sense, Earl?''

Too much sense, he thought bleakly. That was
the price she had to pay for her talent. The fear it
could bring. The temptation to use it, to be sure,
against the temptation not to use, to retain hope.
And how long could the desire simply to hope last
against the desire to know for certain?

''You said something about the ship,'' he said
thoughtfully. ''That you thought something might
be wrong. Would be wrong,'' he corrected. ''What
did you see?''

"Nothing too clear," she said. "Faint images, a lot of them, stars and—"

"Stars? Are you sure?"

"Yes, Earl, but we're in space and surely that's natural."

Wrong, he thought bleakly. From a ship in space stars were the last thing anyone would expect to see. Not with the Erhaft field wrapping the cocoon of metal in its own private universe and allowing it to traverse the spaces between worlds at multi-light speeds. Stars could not be seen beyond that field. If she saw them it could only mean that, somehow, the field had collapsed. But when? When?

"Look," he said, suddenly worried. "Look now. Concentrate. Tell me what you see an hour from now."

"I can't, Earl. I told you. I don't know just how far I can visualize. Not with any degree of accuracy. A few seconds, even a few minutes, but after that I can't tell with any certainty. That's what frightened me. We aren't together and we should be. We should be!"

"Steady!" He gripped her shoulders, holding her close, trying to dampen her incipient hysteria. "The images were faint, weren't they?" He waited for her nod. "That means they showed an alternate future of a low degree of probability. Now be calm. We'll try an experiment. Think of this cabin. Concentrate. What do you see?"

She closed her eyes, frowned. "The cabin," she said. "Empty."

"Clear?"

"Yes, Earl."

"Try again. Aim further. Still the cabin?"

She nodded. "Still empty and very clear."

He looked around, frowning. This wasn't getting them very far. If only there had been a calendar clock hanging on the bulkhead instead of a mirror it might have helped. The mirror?

"Try again," he said. "Concentrate on the mirror. Can you see a reflection in it?"

"No."

"Not even the door? Is it open or closed?"

"Open."

So they had left the cabin and gone somewhere, leaving the door open. But when? She could be scanning a few minutes from now or even across the space of months to when the compartment waited for a new occupant.

"Earl," said Kalin suddenly. "Something's happening. There's a light in the corridor outside."

He turned, saw the closed door, realized that she was still looking ahead, telling of what was yet to come.

"A light," she continued. "It's getting brighter and—" She screamed, horribly, mouth gaping so that he could see her tongue, the warm redness of her throat. Her hands lifted, clamped to her eyes. "Earl! Earl, I'm blind! Blind!"

"No," he said. "You can't be."

She moaned from behind the shield of her hands.

"Kalin, look at me. Damn you, look at me!" Dumarest tore the hands from her face, stared into her eyes. "It hasn't happened yet," he said slowly, giving emphasis to each word. "Whatever it was is still to come. So it can't have affected your sight. You're not blind. Do you understand? You're not blind, Kalin. You can't be."

"Earl!"

"Look at me," he insisted. "What did you see? What happened. Tell, me. Damn you, girl, tell me!"

His harshness was a slap across the face. She looked at him, wonderingly, then shuddered.

"There was a burst of light," she said. "Hard, cold, greenish blue. It was terrible. It burned through my eyes and seared my brain. It wiped out the whole universe." She began to cry. "I mean that, Earl. It wiped out everything. Me, you, everything. There was nothing left after that. Nothing at all!"

A spark of fire, minute, almost imaginary against the dull metal of the lock and then slowly, almost imperceptibly, the panel began to slide open. Sara halted it with the pressure of a hand.

Time, she thought. I must have time. Time to ease the pounding of her heart, to allow over-tensed nerves to relax—to allow the sick horror born when the lock had failed to immediately respond to the key to fade a little. She thinned her lips as she thought of the key. Elmo had provided it at the cost of a clerk for a year. If she had known nothing of electronics the door would have remained sealed. As it was the thing had barely worked after her third adjustment.

Had Elmo intended for her to be caught at the door?

Suspicion clawed at her mind. If the mercentary intended to sell her out, take a reward for warning the crew of intended piracy— She tasted the bile rising in her throat, the released adrenaline stimulating anger and fear. Then the philosophy of a lifetime worked its calm. If he had sold her out they would die together. And, with the decision, came logical thought.

Elmo would not betray her. Like herself he had too much to lose. They must trust each other now or go down in ruin.

She tensed, removed her hand, allowed the panel to slide open. Below lay the interior section of the vessel. The place where the cargo was stored, the rations—the cold region with its glaring ultraviolet tubes and barren sterility. Down here, also, were the power-stacks, the atomic generator and accumulators—the protected muscles of the ship.

Protected, but not by men. There were telltales, warning devices, automatic governors, sensory scanning devices giving three-ply preventative coverage. There would also be an on-duty engineer, his assistant and the handler for those traveling Low. He came to the door, blinking, eyes widening as he saw the woman.

"My lady!" He lifted a hand in protest as she stepped through the opening. "You cannot—"

He froze as the spray hit his palm, dropping into quick-time, turning almost into legendary stone. Quickly Sara closed the panel behind her. It could not be locked but closed, it could delude; open, it could not. She walked through the cold place, not looking at the ranked caskets, the dim figures of their occupants beneath the frosted transparencies. A door led to a passage, a cubicle, a man asleep beneath a dream-helmet, smiling as he enjoyed vicarious pleasure provided by the taped analogue. She left him, still asleep, still smiling, but no longer able to enjoy a dream speeded beyond appreciation.

She too was smiling as she went in search of the third man. It had been so easy. So very easy. Elmo had been proved correct right down the line. Spacemen were overconfident, too certain that no one would dare to take what they commanded, so sure that a few locked doors would keep their passengers safely confined.

The doors were mainly psychological, she realized. A strong man, a strong woman could burst them down and gain the freedom of the vessel. The rest was simplicity itself to any accustomed to violence—if they knew what to do with their gain.

A hand gripped her wrist. Fingers dug into the flesh at the back of her neck. A voice grated harshly in her ear.

"That's just about far enough. Now drop the hypogun before I break your wrist."

She gulped and opened her hand. The instrument made a soft thudding as it landed on the plastic coated floor. She rolled her eyes and caught a glimpse of a thin, intent face, a tattooed insignia. The engineer had been waiting to one side of an opening. Desperation dictated her reaction.

"Let me go!" she croaked. "You're hurting me. If you don't let me go this instant I'll report you to the captain."

Amazement slackened his grip on her neck.

Sara turned to face him. "Are you the engineer? Do you realize that something is wrong? The door is open and a man is lying on the floor. There's blood all over him. I—" She swayed, a frail, painted old woman suddenly devoid of strength.

Contemptuously he released her neck, stooped to pick up the dropped hypogun. One shot and the old bag would be in storage ready for the captain to decide her fate.

He screamed as her elbow rammed into his kidney, a wash of pain filling his eyes with red hazes, his mouth with the taste of blood. He straightened as she kicked the hypogun out of his reach and screamed again as her thumb found his eye. Blinded, almost insane with pain and rage, he reached out, found her body, struck and felt bone snap beneath the edge of his palm. He struck again as her fingers closed on his carotids, again as oblivion rose about his reeling brain, a third time as it closed over his awareness.

Coughing, spraying blood from punctured lungs, Sara staggered from the slumped body of the engineer and sank to her knees.

Three, she thought. Three times the bastard hit me. Where did he learn to hit like that? I should have stayed away from him, let him roar, found the spray and let him have it. Instead I lost my head and closed in. Got within reach and let him smash my ribs, drive them into my lungs, a bunch of splintered knives to rip out my life.

I was careless, she told herself. Stupidly over-confident. He must have been warned about the door opening. A register would have told him—those in the upper regions too—and all he did was to wait for me to walk into his trap.

Elmo too? Had he also walked into a trap? Was he, like her, tasting his own blood, waiting for approaching death?

They'll fix me up, she thought. They'll find me and freeze me and make me almost as good as new. And then, when I'm all healthy again, they'll hold ship's court and I'll be evicted with ten hours' air. A suit and enough dope to make every damn second a nightmare of agony. Me and Elmo. The both of us. What a hell of a way to end.

But there was a better way. Cleaner. The power source was down here and she knew a little about electronics. Enough to do what had to be done. Enough to blow the guts out of the ship and find a clean ending.

Painfully, coughing, leaving a trail of blood on the sterile floor, she crawled down toward the muscles of the ship.

"Now!" Dumarest pressed hard on the ampul, driving it against his skin, triggering the mechanism so that the drug it contained entered his blood. Beside him Kalin followed his example. She gasped as it took effect, her metabolism suddenly jerked into normal speed.

"Earl!"

"Are you all right?" He was anxious; the shock could sometimes prove fatal.

"Yes."

"Good. Now try again." He waited as she closed her eyes and tried to isolate a moment of future time. In his chair the steward looked at his whispering book with dead, unseeing eyes. Irritably Dumarest switched off the page. "Anything?"

"No. Just the glare as before."

"Any fainter images?"

"No."

So the explosion was going to happen and nothing either of them had yet done had altered that probable future. Perhaps it couldn't be altered, not with the facilities at their disposal. Dumarest glanced around the cubicle. The open medical kit he had raided for the emergency antidote to quick-time stood on a shelf. He rummaged through it, stuffing the contents into his pocket, thinking as he worked.

Was the explosion, if that was what the glare would be, caused by internal or external causes? If the latter there was nothing he could do to prevent it. If the former he had a choice. To head for the upper regions and warn the captain or to head for the lower and warn the engineer. If he could only calculate the time it was going to happen.

"I'm going to warn the captain," he told the girl. "Keep checking the future."

He left the cubicle, walked down the passage, halted at her cry.

"Earl!"

"What is it?"

She came running toward him, eyes huge with shock, trembling so that her voice quivered on the edge of total loss of control. "Earl! It's so bright, so close! Just the glare and nothing else. Earl!"

"The cards!" He gripped her shoulders, dug in his fingers, used pain to combat hysteria. "You remember when we played with the cards. The image was clear then. Is it the same now?"

She nodded and he felt the constriction of his stomach. So close? The cards had been scant seconds away in time. Just how long did they have?

The lounge was thirty feet across. Dumarest crossed it in five strides, jerked open a panel flushing the wall, caught the girl's wrist and dragged her into the revealed opening. More doors and they stood in a chill place, dimly lit, a plastic sac open before them. He thrust her inside, sealed the container, paused with his hand on the material. Beyond it a control protruded from the wall of the vestibule.

"Once more," he urged. "Kalin, try once more—and be certain."

He saw the terror on her face, the squeezing of her eyes, the lifting of her hands to protect them from the searing glare. The control moved beneath his hand. A metal shield gasped as air blasted them from the vestibule. Grayness, thick, opaque, tormented with eye-twisting writhings closed around them.

"Earl!" A form in the grayness: soft, warm, scented with femininity. Hair brushed his cheek as arms closed around his neck. "Earl!"

"It's all right," he soothed. "We've left the ship.

We're outside, still caught in the Erhaft field, still moving along with the vessel. This is an emergency sac," he explained. "It—"

"Earl!"

He gripped her close, closing his eyes, burying his face in the masking softness of her hair as the universe exploded in a glare of greenish blue light. The writhing grayness vanished, burned away, dissolving to be replaced by a ball of dwindling flame. Around them the membrane of the sac puffed, stiffened from internal pressure, the thin skin all that stood between them and the cold hostility of space.

"Earl?" She moved against his chest. "It's gone, Earl. The glare. Shall I look to see what will happen next?"

"Not yet." Ampuls glittered as he fumbled them from his pocket. The normal drugs carried by any ship. Compounds to defeat pain, to ensure sleep, to kill time. He used the latter two and looked at her as the lids closed over the green eyes.

Quick-time to slow down her metabolism and drugged sleep so that she could avoid the torment of speculation, the temptation to stare into a future, which, logically, could not exist.

Not for people stranded in an emergency sac between the stars.

He shifted a little, cradling the flame tinted head on his shoulder, conscious of the silken glow of naked flesh, the smooth skin of arms and chest and long, long thighs. Beyond the transparent membrane the stars blazed with scintillating colors. The light shone and sparkled so that it dazzled and touched everything with silver. The sac, his clothes, her tunic, her hair—

Silver and red and an elfin face. The scent of femininity and the warmth of someone close.

The prick of needles brought slowing and sleep.

V

IN THE DIM LIGHT beyond the mesh the man's face was drawn, strained. "Grant me forgiveness, Brother, for I have done much wrong."

Sitting behind the mesh, Brother Jerome listened to the litany of wrongdoing and mentally stepped back half a century in time, and forgotten light-years in distance, to when he had helped to establish a church on an inhospitable world. They had been hard days, hard enough to test the resolution of a man who had, until then, never known real hardship. Well, he had survived and in ways he no longer cared to think about. He had seen the human animal at its worst; the human angel at its best. Two sides of the same coin. If he could enhance one at the expense of the other, it would be enough.

". . . and, Brother, I was jealous of my friend. He had a new house and I lied about my circumstances and . . ."

Sins like stones rolling from a basically decent soul. Basically decent because otherwise the man would not be here, not be suffering the anguish of overwhelming guilt. It was good to know that that anguish, at least, could be resolved.

Brother Jerome switched on the benediction light as the voice ceased. The face was tense, the eyes hungry with anticipation as the swirling kaleidoscope of color caught and held his attention.

"Look into the light of forgiveness," said the monk softly. "Bathe in the flame of righteousness and be eased of all pain, cleansed of all sin. Yield to the benediction of the Universal Brotherhood."

The light was hypnotic, the subject susceptible, the monk an old master of his craft. The face relaxed and peace smoothed the features. Subjectively the man was undergoing self-determined penance. Later he would receive the bread of forgiveness.

The High Monk stretched as he left the booth. Today he had chosen to spend his hour of relaxation at the confessionals and wondered if he had done so simply in order to recapture his youth. It was probable, he admitted on his way back to his office. There was no harm in looking back as long as it was kept in mind that events moved forward. And it was good to know that he still served a purpose, that he could still give a man ease of heart.

Brother Fran looked up as Jerome entered the inner chamber. The secretary held a folder of papers in his hand. He rested it on the desk. "There is news from Sard, Brother."

"With reference to Centon Frenchi?"

"Yes."

Jerome seated himself and looked at the folder without touching it. "His story, of course, has been verified in every detail."

"As you said it would be."

"It was a minor prediction," said Jerome quietly. "I didn't doubt for a moment that the facts as he gave them would tally with the facts we might discover in an independent investigation. Even so, the man was lying."

Brother Fran made no comment.

Jerome raised his eyebrows. "You do not agree?"

"The facts as he gave them have proved to be true," said the secretary cautiously. "But," he admitted, "facts can be both manufactured and manipulated. Yet, in this case—"

"Look at the facts," interrupted the High Monk. "The details. That there was an actual vendetta I do not for one moment question. The daughter, he claims, left the planet years ago. With all the family dead who is there to verify that statement? But it could be true. Stranger things have happened and he certainly has an excellent reason for trying to find the girl. And yet I am not satisfied. Something does not ring true."

"The likeness," said Brother Fran. "It is an inconsistency."

"It is more than that," said Jerome evenly. "Would he have kept it for five years? Perhaps. But, in that length of time a girl can change. Is her hair still red? Her eyes still green? Her measurements, certainly, need not be the same. And yet he mentioned nothing of this." His fingers made little rapping sounds as he drummed them on the folder. "Her coloring," he mused. "Is it not unusual for Sard?"

"Unusual but not unknown," said the secretary. "Red-haired women married into several of the higher families several generations ago. The pure strain has become diluted but there are instances of atavists. The girl could be such a one. A throwback to her early ancestry."

"Or," said Jerome slowly, "that could be yet another manipulated fact. Several worlds have bred for these peculiar characteristics. The girl could have originated on one of those and not on Sard at all." He looked sharply at the other monk. "You think that I am being too suspicious?"

"I think that caution can be carried to the point where it loses its value."

"Yet you agree there are inconsistencies?"

"Everything is open to doubt," said the secretary flatly. "But we must be logical. What point would there be in Centon Frenchi lying to us? Either he wants to find the girl or he does not. His positive action in coming to us to beg our aid proves that he does want to find her."

"I have never doubted that for one second," said the High Monk quietly.

Brother Fran restrained his impatience. "Then,

surely, the only question now remaining is whether we look for her or not.''

"You think so?" Jerome shook his head. "That is not the question at all. Whether we look for her or not is something already decided—we do. Already we are looking. But the real question remains. Assuming that Centon Frenchi is lying, and instinct tells me that he is, just what reason has he for wanting to find her? Or," he added after a moment's pause, "is he working for someone else?"

"And, if so, for whom?"

"Exactly," said Brother Jerome. "An intriguing situation, is it not?"

A shadow drifted from the clouds, circled, wide-winged and silent. It straightened and became a hundred pound projectile of flesh and feather tipped with eighteen inches of tapering bone. Kramm watched it come, lifted his rifle and stared through the telescopic sight. Gently he closed his finger on the trigger. The explosion made a sharp crack echoed by another, more distant and muffled. The thren twitched as the explosive bullet ripped its interior to shreds. The long beak opened in a soundless gesture of pain; then another shot filled the air with once-living debris.

Beneath him the horse moved once, then quietened to the pressure of his knees.

"A good shot, master." Elgin, the verderer, spat in the direction of the thren. "That's one monster who will never raid our herds again. More's the pity that you could not destroy them all with a single bullet from your rifle. There is none on Solis more likely to do that than yourself. Never have I seen a better marksman.''

The praise was extravagant, overly so, but Elgin was currying favor and Kramm knew why. The man had his eye on a girl of the household. Kramm knew that she was not adverse to changing the duties of the kitchen for those of a wife. Provided their genes matched, so that the color bred true, there was no barrier to their union. But it pleased him to keep the man on edge. It would even pay the girl later dividends. No man valued what came too easily.

"He never misses," said Elgin to the third member of the party. "Fives times now he has won the challenge head at the open competition."

"That's enough," said Kramm.

"I but speak what all men know, master."

"Our guest is not concerned with local gossip," said Kramm. "Let us be on our way."

Scarlet fabric rippled as the horses began to move. The cyber, Kramm guessed, was having trouble keeping in the saddle, but the thin expressionless face beneath the cowl gave no sign of any difficulty. Kramm almost yielded to the temptation to break into a gallop; then sternly resisted it. Cyber Mede was not a person with whom to jest. Neither was the Cyclan an organization at which to sneer. Too many had gained too much for that.

"My apologies that you must travel in so primitive a manner," he said after scanning the sky for sight of a wheeling shadow. It had become almost instinctive, this searching of the clouds. "To ride a

beast of burden must be a novel experience for
you."

"It is, but do not blame yourself, my lord."
Mede's voice was a trained modulation devoid of
all irritant factors. "I could have chosen to wait for
a flier. Instead I decided to accompany you. You
breed horses, my lord?"

"The finest on the planet," said Kramm without
boasting. "A pure strain which has yet to be
equaled in this sector of space. Unfortunately the
thren find them succulent prey." His eyes lifted to
the sky. "One day I'll band some men and burn out
their nests."

"Is that possible, my lord?"

"No," admitted Kramm. "It's been tried before. Too many breeding spots and not enough
men, but one day we'll do it."

"Radioactive dusts could help, my lord. In the
meantime why do you not protect your beasts with
lasers?"

"Lasers cost money, cyber." Kramm guided
his mount between two boulders. "On Solis
money is scarce. We raise horses, dairy herds,
some fruit and grain. We manufacture small items
of little cost and limited appeal. I make my own
powder and load my own shells."

He shrugged, dismissing the subject, conscious
of all that he had left unsaid. But how to communi-
cate with a man who was a total stranger to all
emotion? How to describe the thrill attending the
use of a rifle? The kick of the butt, the clean, sharp
sound of the shot, the satisfaction of hitting the
target and seeing feathers fly?

They wended on between boulders and rising slopes. The horses merged into the background as the sky began to dull. Sleek shapes, maned, tailed, anachronisms in an age where ships spanned the stars and power came in portable units. Only the three splotches of flaming color gave the scene brightness and life. The robe of the cyber and the hair of the two other men. Red hair of a peculiar flame-like brilliance. The hallmark of the people of Solis.

Kramm turned in his saddle, eyes raking the sky before he lowered them to the cyber. In the gathering twilight his skin shone nacreous. Behind him, green eyes watchful, Elgin scanned the surrounding slopes, the empty clouds.

"How are you doing, cyber?" Kramm's voice rose in echoes from the dunes. "Have you discovered yet how to turn this scrub into wealth?"

"The problems of a planet are not so easily solved, my lord," said Mede smoothly. "Will the journey last much longer?"

"Getting sore?" Kramm's laugh came from his belly, rolling, deep. "Take no offense, cyber, you've done better than most could have managed in your place." He laughed again. "You'll have reason to remember Klieg. Our house," he explained. "The founder called it that. A long time ago now."

Long enough to breed a race of green-eyed, pale-skinned men and women with heads of flame. Pride, thought Mede detachedly. A poor planet, yet a proud one. A world made almost unique by the founders. Almost. Solis was not the only planet on which red hair was dominant.

An hour later they rounded a curve and came within sight of the house. Mede stared at it from beneath the shadow of his cowl. Stone walls enclosing a courtyard. Thick walls of stone rising within to support a sloping roof. There would be snow here in the winter, he knew. Snow and heavy ice. Only in one thing was the house different from a dozen others he had seen during his stay on the planet. Its proximity to the sea. It clung to the cliff, one side facing the water, a limpet defying nature.

Kramm grunted as his horse, scenting its stable, broke into a canter.

"Steady, girl," he said. "Steady." And then, to Mede. "Home, cyber. Welcome to Klieg."

Komis heard the music as he opened the door of his study. It shrilled high, clear and far too loudly. The skirl of pipes echoed above the rattle of drums. Keelan's favorite, the tune which she had hummed and sang and played all the time when Brasque was away. The tune which they had composed together and played at their wedding and played even after that dreadful time when the universe had turned against their happiness. The tune which had turned into a dirge and which he hadn't heard for a long time now.

The stairs fell away beneath his feet. The music swelled even louder as he reached the door, opened it, stepped into the room with the open side, with the sea-scent and sea-wind coming through the pillars. Another door and a white-faced girl dancing with her red hair a swirling flame.

"Mandris!"

"Master!" She turned, shock widening her green eyes, hands lifting to cover her mouth. Against one wall the record player spilled its music, the speakers sonorous with over-amplification. "Master, I—"

He reached her, passed her, killed the music with a twist of his strong white fingers. He stood in the abrupt silence, ears strained, listening—looking toward the shadowed room past an open door, the darkened room where Keelan lay.

Silence. Nothing but what had been for too long now. He turned and stared at the shame-faced girl. She cringed before his eyes.

"Master! I am sorry! I did not think. But it grows so silent here, so lonely. I thought that—"

"You did not think," he interrupted coldly. "There could have been a cry, an appeal for aid. Could you have heard it over that noise?" The thought of it generated rage, a mounting, consuming anger. "Your duty is to serve," he said. "To wait, to watch, to listen. To attend the Lady Keelan at all times. For this we give you money for your dowry."

She lowered her eyes, pink flushing the pearl of her cheeks.

"But you grew bored. You decided to play a little music. To play and dance and, perhaps, to dream of a strong young lover riding to carry you away." He caught himself. He was being petty, unfair. Of what else should a young girl dream? And yet she must learn her lesson. "If I gave you the choice, which would you choose?" he snapped. "Dis-

charge from our service or twenty lashes on the
naked back?'' Again he was being unfair. Discharge would mean degradation, the loss of status,
the opportunity to better her position. And yet
who would willingly be lashed?

"Never mind," he said quickly before she could
answer.

"Master?"

He was not a consciously cruel man. Punishment, if it was to be given, should be announced
immediately. To delay was to be sadistic and her
fault had been no more than human frailty. He
looked around the chamber. It was too silent, too
somber for someone so young. Beyond the outer
door the sea-sound echoed. Inside the inner door
only darkness and the knowledge of what lay
within. And, who knew that the music might not
have been a stimulus? Perhaps they were wrong to
maintain such a stringent watch.

"Your ears need attention, my girl," he said.
"Such a noise would earn you a beating if it woke
your man." He caught her frown, the pucker of
her lips. Irony was wasted here. "It was too
loud," he said pointedly. "Far too loud. It could
be heard all over the house."

"I am sorry, master."

"Sorrow mends no dishes," he said. "See that it
does not happen again."

"Yes, master."

He hesitated, a little ashamed of his reluctance,
then stepped to the open inner door and peered
within. Nothing but the gloom and the solitary
lamp glowing like an emerald in the shadows. At

least she was still alive, and if he did not see her, he
could cling to the illusion aroused by the music.
The memory of love and beauty and wonderful
grace. An illusion that a light now would totally
destroy.

Sighing, he turned away and heard the signal
bell announcing the arrival of his brother and their
guest.

Kramm lifted his goblet, drank deep, slammed it
down and wiped the froth from his upper lip. A
litter of gnawed bones lay on the plate before him.
In Kramm the barbarian lurked very close to the
surface. He snapped his fingers at a serving girl
and helped himself to pastry. His laughter rolled as
he held out his goblet for more beer.

"Good food, good drink," he said. "What did I
promise you, cyber? That and more, yes?" He
drank, not waiting for an answer. "A warm room
and a soft bed. Something to fill it and life is complete."

"For some, perhaps, my lord," agreed Mede.
He sat upright at his place, the remains of a frugal
meal on his plate, his beer untouched. His cowl
rested on his shoulders, its protection unnecessary
in the heat of the room. In the light his shaven head
had the appearance of a skull.

"For all," insisted Kramm. The beer had edged
his tongue. "Fill the man's belly, keep his body
cool, his mind calm and you have a contented soul.
You now—picking at your food, sipping water instead of good, wholesome beer—think of what
you miss." He waved his goblet at the cyber. "But

it's your loss, not mine. A toast," he roared. "To our guest. To the Cyclan!"

A dozen goblets rattled empty to the board. Komis rose from his seat at the head of the table. "Many of our ways are without polish," he said to Mede. "But our welcome is from the heart."

Mede bowed. "You are gracious, my lord."

"We are grateful," corrected Komis. He resumed his chair. "For the help which you so freely offer and which we could never afford." He paused and the cyber picked up the bait.

"Solis is a world with high potential, my lord. It may be possible to realize that potential. If so, it may be that the rulers of this place would be eager to retain the services of the Cyclan."

It seemed logical enough and it was foolish to look a gift horse in the mouth, but Komis wished that the cyber had betrayed more of the human weakness inherent in men. He was too cold, too remote, too like a machine. But that, of course, the head of Klieg reminded himself, was exactly what the cyber was.

When young he had been chosen. At early adolescence, after a forced puberty, he had undergone an operation on the emotional center of the brain. He could feel no joy, no pain, no hate, no desire. He was a coldly logical machine of flesh and blood, a living robot—detached, passionless. The only pleasure he could ever know was the mental satisfaction of having made a correct deduction, of seeing his predictions fulfill themselves.

"Tell me, Mede," he said, more to put the guest at ease than from real interest. "You chose to ride to Klieg. Did you see anything which could be improved?"

"I lack true data to make an accurate prediction, my lord Komis," said Mede smoothly. "But I would venture to say that the depredations of the threns grow at a worrying rate of increase. It would be a safe prediction to state that, unless circumstances alter, your herds have reached their maximum possible numbers. In fact, they are already on the decrease."

"How did you know that?" Kramm roared from where he sat at the table. "How could you know?"

"Your range is wide, your men few, the predators many. Any life-form given a continual and easily obtainable source of food will increase to the maximum numbers that food will support. Using the primitive weapons you do, it is impossible to kill them in sufficient quantities to control their numbers. They breed faster than they can be killed. You admitted that you could not destroy their breeding places," the cyber reminded the purpling Kramm. "The prediction then is simply a matter of extrapolation. Overbreeding will increase the attacks of the thren on your herds. Larger numbers will make them at first vulnerable, but those same numbers will cause greater depredations among your cattle. The numbers will thin and a balance be struck. But, always, the advantage lies with the predators. You simply cannot afford enough men to watch the skies. Only when the herd is small enough for your men to protect will the curve level out.''

"And how large will the herd be then?'' asked Komis.

Mede hesitated. "I lack data,'' he admitted. "The final size, however, depends on the number of men available for guard duty which, in turn, depends on the profit-ratio between horse and keep. If it takes the profit from ten beasts to keep one man then only one man at most can be available for guard. In fact the ratio is less than that because a man must sleep, be fed, housed, supplied with equipment. The ratio is usually two to one—two men working to keep one in the field.''

Komis nodded as Mede fell silent. The figures in the books lying on the desk in his study told the same grim story. Rising costs against lowered income and the more one rose, the lower the other fell.

Kramm managed to find his voice. "Primitive weapons!'' he shouted. "I can pick the eye from a thren at a hundred yards. More. You object to my using a rifle?''

Mede's voice remained the same even modulation. "I do not object, my lord. I do not oppose. I do not aid. I take no sides. I am of value only while I remain detached. I advise; nothing more.''

Komis waved his brother to silence. "What do you suggest we do?''

"The life cycle of the thren should be thoroughly checked to see that it is not essential to the ecology of the planet. If it is not, then radioactive dusts should be scattered on the nesting sites."

Kramm snorted. "Radioactive dusts cost money, cyber."

"The outlay would be recovered by stock not lost, my lord. By men not wasted in searching the clouds."

Komis rose, ending the discussion. "It is late," he announced. "You have ridden far and must be tired. Kramm, show our guest to his room."

He was alone when Kramm returned, sitting at the head of the table, staring thoughtfully into space. He rose and together they mounted the stairs to where the sea-sound and sea-scent swept through the pillars of the open-sided room. Kramm glanced at the closed door behind which a girl sat in attendance.

"The same?"

Komis nodded.

"I would go in but—" Kramm shook his head. "On the way here," he said, "riding through the valley, I thought of her. It used to be her favorite place." His hands closed, knotted. "Keelan," he said. "Our sister."

Leaning on the parapet, he stared down into darkness, down to where the surge and suck of waves washed the granite teeth of the rocks far below.

VI

A VEINED DISC shattered, became eyes, nose, a mouth and graduated chins. A voice like the shrill squeak of slate dragged over a nail. "... teach you to obey! You ain't no kid of mine, so don't go thinking you are! Young varmint! Take that ... and that ... and ..."

The woman vanished. Light splintered into a new visage: rheumy eyes, slack mouthed, spittle drooling from a slimy beard. "... never been right since his folks died. Shouldn't have taken him in but figured give him chance to earn his keep. Only thing now is to thrash sense into him or sell him to farm. Sell ... sell ... sell."

The impact of blows, the pain, the rising red tide of murderous anger. Scenes jumped like a tape skittering in its guide: red desert, white moonlight,

the yellow flicker of dancing flame. Taste sensa-
tions: the sting of spines, the sweetness of water,
the rich soup of blood, the stringy chewsomeness
of freshly killed meat. Mental emotion images:
loneliness and fear and constant alertness. Physical discomfort. Fear. Hunger. Pain. Fear. Loneliness. Hunger. Fear. Hunger. Hunger.

A spaceship like a glittering balloon dropping
from the skies.

Furred beasts. Rabbits. Rats. Snarling dogs.
Scaled things: lizards, snakes, creatures which
spat. Spiders and beetles and things that scuttled
and lurked beneath stones.

Hunger. Thirst. Hunger. Thirst. Hunger.
Hunger. Hunger.

Another ship falling like a spangled leaf.

"No!" said Dumarest. "No!"

Hands gripped his shoulders, hard, firm;
stroboscopic light flashed into his eyes. The tang
of something acrid strutted his reeling senses.

Dumarest gasped. "What—?"

"You were dreaming," said a voice. "You are all
right now."

The hands fell away, the flashing died, a cabin
swam into view. Metal and crystal and sterile plastic. Cabinets and familiar machines. A man with a
smooth round head and a tunic of medical green
neatly closed high around his throat. He smiled as
Dumarest struggled to sit upright.

"You can relax now," he said. "You've got
nothing to worry about. A little disorientation but
that will pass. Will you answer a question?"

"What do you want to know?"

"Your dreams. They were of the past, when you were very young. Right?"

Dumarest blinked his surprise at the question. "Yes."

"It's always the same," said the man. "You had prepared for death," he explained. "Logically you could expect nothing else, but you have a strong survival factor and your ego, in trying to avoid extinction, sought escape in the past." He shrugged. "It happens all the time. The ones I worry about are those who don't dream at all."

"Then don't worry about me," said Dumarest. He looked around the room. "Where is she?"

"The girl?" The medic pointed to a screen. "She's taking her time about rejoining the human race, but she'll make it." He caught Dumarest by the arm as he stepped toward the screen. "I said that she'd make it."

Dumarest jerked free his arm and swept aside the screen. Kalin lay supine, the light gleaming from her golden tunic, glowing warm in the mane of her hair. For a moment he thought she was dead, then he saw the slow rise of her chest, saw the pulse of blood in the great arteries of her throat.

"I told you that she was all right," said the medic. "She's just a little slow in snapping out of it." He reached forward and gently slapped her cheek. "How much sleepy-dope did you give her?"

"How do you know I gave her any?"

"I saw you brought in. There were empty ampuls by your hand and, anyway, who else would have given her medication?" The medic's voice held impatience. "Well, how much did you give her?"

"A couple of shots."

"And quick-time?"

"A regular dose."

"That's what I figured. Well, a little stimulation won't do any harm." The medic triggered his hypogun. Eyelashes lifted from pearl-like cheeks as the green eyes opened. They were blank windows without expression or recognition.

"Kalin!" Dumarest stooped over her, his shadow darkening her face. "It's all right," he said. "We've been picked up and we're both alive and well."

She blinked and opened her mouth as if to scream. Then, suddenly, the eyes snapped to full life. She lifted her arms and closed them around his neck.

"Earl, darling! Earl!"

"Steady," he said gently. "Steady."

She blazed with the joy of resurrection, the realization that she was alive and safe and had nothing to fear. He knew how she felt. How everyone traveling Low felt when the needles bit and the eddy currents warmed and the caskets opened like a reluctant grave.

A buzzer sounded from a speaker set high against a wall. A warm, lilting voice followed the discordant note. "Medical?"

The medic looked at the instrument. "Sir!"

"How are your patients? Are they recovered yet?"

"Almost, sir."

"Send them to me immediately they are able to walk."

The medic shrugged as he met Dumarest's eyes. "You heard the man."

"I heard him." Dumarest helped the girl from the couch, gripped her hand as she stood at his side. "Are you going to tell us what happened or do you want to leave it to the boss?"

"As you say," said the medic drily. "He's the boss."

He wore blue and green with touches of yellow and points of scarlet. A slim, long-faced man with jet black hair and fingers richly crusted with gems. He lounged in a chair behind a wide desk made of shimmering crystal: on the surface of it mechanical chessmen went through the maneuvers of a recorded game.

He looked a little like a clown, a dandy, a spoiled darling of a favored world. He smiled as they entered and gestured to chairs. "Be seated," he said. "My name is Argostan. Yours?"

Dumarest gave them.

"You are curt," said Argostan. "You give me your names and nothing more. Have you no home? No family? No business?"

"We are travelers," said Dumarest. "Of no settled world."

"You perhaps," said the gaudily dressed man. His eyes glowed as he looked at the girl. "You bear the mark of a hundred suns, but Kalin? She is no traveler. A gypsy, perhaps. A star gypsy.

Have you known each other long?"

"Long enough," she said, and gripped Dumarest by the arm.

Argostan smiled. "So you have formed an attachment? That is good. I like to see people who have a meaning for each other. Life is barren unless there is someone to share its pain and pleasure. You will join me in wine?" He passed them glasses without waiting for an answer and lifted his own. "A toast," he said. "Let us drink to the combination of favorable circumstances known as luck. Good luck," he emphasized. "Let us drink to that."

The wine was sweet, slightly astringent, delicately flavored.

"If you took all the luck that is due to a normal man," mused Argostan, "multiplied it by a factor of ten to the tenth power and then doubled it to embrace you both, you would have used it all in one go. Can either of you imagine the odds against having been rescued?"

"Yes," said Dumarest flatly. "I can."

Argostan looked at him sharply. "Tell me what happened," he said. "Omit no detail." He blinked when Dumarest had finished and slowly poured them all more wine.

"There was an accident," he said. "The engineer managed to give warning that the engines were about to explode. You were fortunate in that you were being shown the emergency sac by the steward. Before you knew it, he had thrust you inside and tripped the release."

"We were lucky," said Dumarest.

"More than you can possibly realize." Argostan sipped a little wine. "Had I been in your position, I would have chosen to remain with the vessel. At least it would have been a quick death. To drift, sealed in that plastic bag, aware of the incredibly hopeless chance of rescue—" He shook his head. "You made a brave decision."

"We had no chance to make any decision at all," corrected Dumarest sharply. "As I told you, the steward acted on his own volition." He lifted his own glass, sipped, set it down. "It is needless for me to express our thanks to you for having saved our lives. You must know how we feel. Nothing could ever express our appreciation."

"Nothing?" Argostan lifted his eyebrows. "Well, perhaps not." He finished his wine and stared somberly at the maneuvering chessmen. "My captain caught the signal of an explosion on his instruments. He reported it and I was curious. I ordered a search. The beacon of your sac registered and we found you." He smiled. "Put like that, how simple it seems. But how many million cubic miles of space did we comb? The time wasted we can calculate, the expense, but never those reaching miles of emptiness. A less patient man would have abandoned the search long before you were found."

A silence fell, broken only by the small sounds made by the mechanical chessmen. A bishop swept toward a rook and took its place. A pawn left the board. A knight sprang into a new position. The black queen moved relentlessly toward the white king.

"You are trying to say something," said Dumarest. "I fail to discern what it is."

"Really? I would not have taken you to be an obtuse man." The dandy delicately touched his lips with a scrap of lace. "I am in business," he said. "I buy and I sell, and if I cannot buy, I take. We are heading for Chron. Need I say more?"

Kalin sensed the tension. The grip of her fingers matched the urgency of her voice. "Earl. What does he mean?"

"Chron is a mining world," said Dumarest shortly. "Only some factors and supervisors go there willingly. There are some stranded travelers. The rest are slaves."

He heard the sudden intake of her breath, the hiss of comprehension.

"That's right," he said. "Our rescuer is a slaver."

"It is a business," said Argostan. For him the word held no insult. For those needing labor on Chron, the same. It was, as he said, a simple matter of supply and demand. "And I am sure you can appreciate my position. You are worth money." His eyes rested on the girl. "Much money. I cannot neglect the opportunity. And do not be so unfair as to begrudge me a share of your good fortune. If it were not for me, you would be dead. Dust among the stars. Logically, then, surely your lives are mine?"

Dumarest restrained the impulse to throw himself at the dandy's throat. He would be lucky to reach the desk. Automatic weapons would be trained on where he sat. Instead he forced himself to smile. "As a man of business I assume that you are open to an offer?"

Argostan smiled. "A philosopher! This is an unexpected pleasure!"

"I am a realist. How much would you charge me for two High passages to Chron?"

The slaver pursed his lips. "You are strong," he said. "The girl is desirable. Pay me what you would fetch and you arrive free. I keep my word," he added. "You need have no fear of that."

Dumarest rose, stripped off his tunic, bared his left arm. "You have a banking machine?"

It was a foolish question. Any man in Argostan's trade would need instant banking facilities. The desk opened, revealing a machine with a panel and a gaping hole. Without hesitation, Dumarest thrust his arm into the orifice. Clamps seized the limb; electronic devices scanned the metallic inks of the tattoo set invisibly below the skin. A forgery would have resulted in a gush of incinerating flame. That tattoo was genuine. A signal lamp flashed green on the panel as figures showed the amount of credit signified by the brand.

The slaver frowned.

"It is enough," said Dumarest. And then, as the man hesitated. "It is all I have."

Kalin spoke from where she stood watching. "I am ignorant in these matters, but how much is a dead woman worth on Chron?"

Argostan was amused. "You would not be dead," he said. "I am scarcely a novice to this trade. But I admire your spirit." He set the controls of the banker. "I shall not leave you penniless," he said to Dumarest. "I shall leave you"—he paused, thoughtful—"the cost of one half a Low passage."

He pressed the activating switch. Magnetic beams removed the old tattoo, credited the selected amount to Argostan's balance, replaced the old brand with a new one showing the revised amount. The slaver turned, smiling.

"Welcome aboard," he said. "Enjoy yourselves. In three days we land on Chron."

It was a bleak place with thin winds and acrid dust which, in times of storm, blew in vast clouds beneath a copper sky. An amber sun clung sullenly to the horizon and threw exaggerated shadows over the gritty soil.

Kalin lifted her hands to bare shoulders and hugged herself. "Earl, it's cold! Miserable!"

"It's a dead-end world," he said flatly.

"What—?"

"Never mind."

He took her arm and guided her away from a line of men marching from a bulking warehouse to the ship. They wore drab gray striped with scarlet, the glint of metal showing from the collars about their necks, and each man carried an ingot of refined metal: Argostan's payment for the cargo he had delivered. An overseer had already hurried them away. His twin, brilliant in orange cloak and helmet, looked curiously at the pair as Dumarest led the way toward the edge of the field. His eyes lingered on the girl; the whip he carried in his right hand made sharp snapping noises as he lashed the side of his boot.

"You are staying on Chron for reasons of business, sir and madam?" The tout had oily hair, an oily face, a voice to match. "The Hotel Extempore is unequaled on the planet. The administrators themselves reside there when visiting Chron. I will myself carry your baggage."

Dumarest walked past him.

"If the Hotel Extempore is a little too grand, sir and madam, I represent a more modest establishment." The tout ran beside them, looking up into Dumarest's face. "The Albion Rooms are clean, the food is good, the charges reasonable. Your baggage, sir and madam?"

"Get lost," snapped Dumarest.

"There is nowhere to go," said the tout reasonably. "Your ship is the only new arrival and you are the only free passengers. I beg of you to let me be of service. If the Albion Rooms are a little too grand, then may I escort you to Pete's Bar?" He looked at the girl, eyes drifting over her hair, her body. "There is always a welcome at Pete's for those who are willing to help him entertain his friends."

"No!" said Kalin sharply. "Earl, don't!"

Dumarest looked at her.

"You were choking him," she said. "I mean that you are going to choke him. That is—"

"If he doesn't shut his mouth I'll break his neck," said Dumarest flatly. "That's what you mean. This time he's making his proposition to the wrong people.''

The tout backed away. ''My apologies, sir and madam,'' he said quickly. ''No offense was intended. But, on Chron, as everywhere else, a man must eat.''

Dumarest looked at the girl as the tout moved away. ''You shouldn't have done that,'' he said quietly. ''If nothing else, you could have warned the man of what I intended. But you should keep silent for another reason. Sensitives are rarely popular on worlds like this.''

''Is it such a bad world, Earl?''

It was bad enough. A dead-end world at the end of the line. A rolling cinder without a local population, local industry, or native assets. Without opportunity for a man to get a job, build up a stake, get the price of a passage so as to make his escape.

A federation of companies mined the planet. Their gigantic machines gouging deep into the mountains—rivers of power streaming from their atomic plants so as to fuse the buried ore by eddy currents, run it through taps and channels into molds. Second stage was refining the crude pigs, pouring into standard shapes, stacking in warehouses—there to wait for the freighters to come and ship it to the manufacturing worlds. Over the secondary smelters hung a billowing cloud of heat-borne ash. What use a cleaner when there was no one to consider?

Only the technicians, supervisors and overseers were highly paid contract men willing to stand dirt and fumes and rugged conditions for the sake of big rewards. The workers didn't count. Slave-labor. Men who had been sold to pay their debts, who had sold themselves for their families' sakes, who had been kidnapped and stolen and who could do nothing about it.

The rest of the population consisted of stranded travelers, entrepreneurs, entertainers. The inevitable appendages to any community where there is a chance of money to be made or needs to satisfy.

Dumarest halted as they left the field. A rabble stood watching: men shabbily dressed, gaunt, eyes smoldering with desperation or dull with hopeless resignation. The collared slaves were better dressed and in better condition than the stranded. Well to one side, the plastic bubbles which housed the executive quarters shone with lambent light and warmth. Closer, nearer to the landing field, a collection of bubbles, houses made of local stone, sheds with dirt walls and weighed roofs comprised the local village. To the other side, sheltered and almost hidden in a valley was the rubbish dump that was Lowtown.

A muscle tightened in Dumarest's jaw as he looked at it.

"Earl." Kalin tugged at his arm. "Can't we go somewhere warm? I'm getting cold."

He loosened the fastenings of his tunic, doffed it, slipped it around her shoulders. Denied the insulation of the protective material his skin reacted, tightening against the chill. Behind, the sun made no impression; ahead, their shadows sprawled like distorted reflections of monstrous entities.

"We'll find a banker," he decided. "We must get you something warm to wear. A cloak, protective coverings for your feet, a knife."

"A laser would be better." She did not pretend to misunderstand.

"You know how to use a knife," he said gently. "And lasers cost money."

So did boots, a cloak, a knife.

Dumarest looked at the few coins left from their purchase and dropped them into her palm. Kalin looked different. The golden tunic had gone to pay for more appropriate clothing. Her mane of flaming hair coiled beneath the rim of an insulated helmet. Pants, covering her tapering legs, tucked into high boots, belted against a shirt which, in turn, was covered by a rough tunic. The high-collared cloak was marked in zig-zags of green and yellow. The knife was a thin edged, pointed strip of steel carried in a sheath strapped to her left forearm.

She chuckled as they stood in the dust of the main and single street of the village. "You know, Earl, this is fun. I've never worn clothing like this before."

She had never been stranded on a world like Chron before either. Dumarest had. It was an experience he had never wanted to repeat.

VII

A KNOT OF MEN came down a winding path leading from the far end of the village. Dumarest stepped back as they approached. Two of the men carried something shapeless slung on a thick pole, the weight stooping their shoulders. Two others carried packs and supported a third man between them. He clung to their necks, legs trailing in the dust. His face was white beneath the dirt, strained, a thick rope of dried blood ran from the corner of his mouth. The chest of his shabby tunic was stiff with more of the same. The sixth man was big, stocky. The side of his face puckered as if it had been seared with fire.

A man called from the far side of the street. "Any luck, Arn?"

The scarred man spat. "Sure," he said bitterly. "A lot of it. All bad."

Dumarest stepped forward as the knot of men halted before a building. He nodded toward the burden slung on the pole. "You've been hunting," he said. "Is there much game here?"

Arn looked at him, then at the girl. "You want to hire some men to go on a hunt?" He frowned as Dumarest shook his head. "Just curious then, uh? Tourists, maybe?"

"Travelers," corrected Dumarest. "Just arrived and stranded."

"The pair of you?" Arn looked at Kalin. "She your woman?"

"That's right," said the girl.

"Tough," said the scarred man. "For you, that is. Alone you'd have no trouble getting the price of a passage." He scowled as Dumarest tensed. "Relax, mister," he said. "I've had a hard time lately but I can still handle what I have to." His voice was flat, dull, a man trying to reassure himself.

He lifted grim hands, thrust thumbs beneath the straps of the pack he carried, flung it to the ground before the door of the building. It gave a metallic sound and Dumarest caught a gleam of mesh through a rip in the clumsily joined material. The two men carrying the pole stepped forward and lowered their burden. A fanged snout showed from among folds of scaled hide, the coils of a barbed tail.

Arn went to the door, hammered on it, returned to where the rest of the group waited. The wounded man lifted his head, stared about with wild eyes.

"Haran," he said. "I can't feel my legs! I can't feel a damn thing—"

The man supporting him on the left eased his weight a little. "Take it easy," he said. "We'll soon have you comfortable."

"But my legs! Haran! I can't—"

"Shut up," said the man on his right. "Don't keep on about it. Just shut up and let's get you home." He looked at the scarred man. "That all right, Arn?"

"Sure," said the leader. He nodded to the two men with the pole. "You go with them," he said. "Give them a hand. You might as well get the pot started while you're at it." He spat in the dust as they moved away. "Zardle meat! As tough as granite and as tasty as sand but if you can get it down and keep it down the stuff will keep you alive."

Dumarest was thoughtful. "Is that what you were hunting? Something for food?"

Arn nodded.

"Then why leave the tail? That's probably the best part."

"It is, but Pete claims the head, skin and tail in return for lending out his nets." Arn turned from the door as something clicked from within. "You're smart," he said. "To know about the tail. Done much hunting?"

"A little," said Dumarest. "When I've had to. But only for food."

"Sometimes you win a bonus hunting a zardle," said the scarred man. "If you're lucky you might find a zerd. It's a thing like a round ball of stone right smack in their heads almost touching the brain. Some say that it's a sort of tumor made up of tissue and calcium deposits, minerals too. The things shine like stars when you hold them in your hand. That's why the women like them," he explained. "They wear them for jewelry. As long as they rest on the naked skin they glow with an ever-changing shine. Beautiful."

"And expensive," said Kalin.

"You know?"

"I've seen them," she said. "They change color according to the emotion of the wearer. Some men give them as gifts to their mistresses so as to test their sincerity. But," she ended, "I didn't know they came from inside the skulls of beasts."

"You know now," said Arn. He nodded to them both. "Guess I'll be seeing you around."

"Wait a minute," said Dumarest quickly. "You've got a pot going. Can we share in it?"

Arn was curt. "No. We worked to get what's in that pot and we can't afford charity."

"I'm not talking about charity," said Dumarest. "You said the meat was tough. We've got a little money. How about if we supply something to make it tender?" He waited for the man's reluctant nod. "Go down to the store," he said to Kalin. Next to where we bought the clothes. Get some tenderizer."

Arn stared after her as she walked down the street. "A fine woman."

Dumarest nodded.

"Qwen had a woman like that," Arn mused.

"Used to talk about her a lot. Carried a talking likeness of her all the time. God knows why he ever left her." He paused. "We buried it with him."

"Was he with you on the hunt?"

"Him and two more. Nine of us—a lucky number. We could have done without that kind of luck. One of the nets gave way. Three dead and Crin's got a broken spine. Four men lost for the sake of a plateful of stew."

"How about Crin?" asked Dumarest. "Is there a chance of medical treatment?"

"Without money? Not a chance."

"Then why didn't you leave him? Pass him out easy?" Dumarest spoke without emotion. "He wouldn't have known what was going on. Now he's going to lie there and suffer and starve. Is that what you call mercy?"

"He had his brothers with him," said Arn. "The ones who were carrying him." He looked at Dumarest. "What would you have done?"

"Left him there."

"Yes," said Arn slowly. "I guess you would."

It grew colder as the sun dipped lower beneath the horizon. One of the men stirring the contents of the strutted bag that was their caldron looked up and sniffed the air.

"It's getting close to winter," he said. "Too close. If we hope to live through it we'd better get in some fuel."

"Why bother?" A thin piebald stretched his broken boots closer to the fire. "We can go up near the smelter like we did last time.''

''Sure,'' agreed the cook. ''Then the wind changes and another seven of us die from the fumes. Or the guards make a raid and ten more of us wear the collar for 'stealing' their waste heat. No thanks. I'll stay free even if I have to freeze doing it.''

''Free!'' The piebald spat into the fire. In the glow of the flames his mottled face writhed in contempt. ''How the hell are we free? Free to starve? To die?''

''We've got a choice,'' said a man from the shadows. ''We don't have to jump when some overseer thumbs a switch.''

''We don't have to eat their food either,'' snapped the piebald. ''You see that food? Good and rich and filling. They dress decent, too. And live in shelters instead of out here on a junk heap. They even get time for recreation,'' he added. ''And a bit of money to spend.''

The man in the shadows laughed. ''That's right. Facsimile women to spend it on. Surrogate women and surrogate wine. Living it up by spending pretend money on pretended dissipation. Robots to cuddle and chemicals to disorient the senses. But they can't get really drunk. Not that. They've got to keep a clear head for work.'' He laughed again. ''Do you know why they do it? Give the slaves tokens to use as local cash?''

The mutant sneered. ''Tell me.''

''You can't take away a privilege a man hasn't got. So you give him something he doesn't want to lose. The more he hangs onto it, the greater hold you've got over him. Simple.''

"That's right," said the piebald. "Now tell me one society that doesn't operate in exactly the same way. Listen," he said. "I was born on Zell. My folks worked a farm. Half of what they grew was theirs—less taxes. I guess they never saw more than a third of any crop they raised. And you know what? The tax assessors came around and told them they'd have to pay another ten percent. The king was getting married or something. He let them sweat for two days and then came back and told them how lucky they were. They were one of the chosen few to have their taxes cut by five percent. You know what? They were grateful. Grateful!"

"Didn't they know they were still going to pay an extra five percent?"

"Sure they knew. They weren't dumb. Not when it came to figures. But they were so relieved that it was only a five instead of a ten percent increase that they almost kissed the tax assessor's rear."

A man cleared his throat. "I don't get it. What's the point?"

The piebald squinted toward him. "We were talking of the slaves, right?"

"I remember."

"They've got nothing, so they get given a little and want to hang onto it. But my folks weren't slaves. They didn't wear a collar. They had a right to take all they worked for. Instead they were grateful for someone giving them back a little of what was theirs in the first place. I tell you—they worked a damn sight harder than any collar-man I've ever seen. And they paid their own way. They didn't have any quarter-master handing out fresh clothing, a commissary to issue food, a doctor when they were sick, warm quarters to sleep in and someone to worry about keeping them happy so they would work hard. They had to work hard simply in order to eat. My old man never had a drink in his life aside from some slop he brewed himself. My old woman never even heard of perfume. They lived like animals and died the same way." He glared into the fire. "Don't talk to me about being free," he said tightly. "Don't sell me that bill of goods. I know better."

A silence fell around the circle, the bulging sac which held the stew bubbled a little and shed vapor. A wind rose, caught the fire, fanned it to leaping flame. Faces swam from the shadows, eyes glittering, teeth dim behind bearded lips.

"Slavery's not economical," said a voice slowly. "It's cheaper to let people fend for themselves."

"Then why the collar-men on Chron?" demanded another. "I'll tell you why. Slaves don't strike, don't join unions, can't cause trouble. Those running the mines want to be sure of a reliable source of labor. They want to protect their investment. There's big money tied up here."

"So why don't you get some?" yelled the piebald. "If you're so smart why are you stranded?"

"Go to hell!"

"Hell? Man, I'm already there. Didn't you know?"

The tension broke with a laugh. Dumarest stirred, felt someone squat at his side. Arn's face glistened in the firelight, the seared skin taut and glowing. Unconsciously he rubbed it. "Philo been stirring it again?"

"The mutant?"

"That's the one. Sometimes I figure him for a company man trying to talk us into donning the collar. He sure makes out a good case." He sucked at his teeth. "Well, maybe I've got a cure for that."

Dumarest was curious. "What is it?"

"Tell you later," said Arn. "After we've eaten." He lowered his voice. "You'd better leave the girl behind."

"No," said Dumarest. He saw the other's expression. "I couldn't if I wanted to and I don't want to. Not here," he explained. "Not yet. Not until I've learned more about the setup here."

Arn shrugged. "Suit yourself," he said and then called to the man standing beside the pot. "Hey, how about that stew? Let's eat!"

Lowtowns were all the same: places where the unfortunate huddled. Holes scooped from the dirt, shacks made of flimsy scraps giving a little visual privacy and nothing else, unpaved lanes winding between noisome dwellings. Temporary camps where stranded travelers stayed until they could haul themselves upward by their bootstraps. There was no drainage, no sanitation, no running water or available power. There was dust and dirt and smell. Unwashed flesh and ragged clothing. The shared communion of a common misfortune.

Arn lifted his bowl and sucked down the last of his portion. "That was good," he said, smacking his lips. "That tenderizer you contributed, Earl, made all the difference." He yelled to the cook. "Hand me some more."

He had led the hunting team which had provided the meat. Silently the cook refilled his bowl. He hesitated, looking at Dumarest.

"Thanks." He took the replenished bowl, ate, chewing determinedly at the gritty meat. Beside him Kalin shuddered as she looked into her bowl.

"Earl, I can't. This isn't fit for a dog."

"It's food," he said shortly. "Eat."

"But—"

"Eat," he said again. A stranded traveler had no right to be particular, not when he never knew when he would next eat. The stew wasn't good but Dumarest had eaten worse. There were vegetables of a kind—probably those thrown out at the commissary. A slimy thing which could have been some form of root, maybe inedible, but providing bulk and minerals. The flesh of the zardle, water, and something else.

"Dead yeast," said Arn. "They run a small brewery in the village and Philo managed to get the dumped slime from the bottom of the vats." He gulped and belched. "It sure gives it body." He hesitated, then put aside the battered container. "No," he decided. "I don't want to get soft. Get my stomach used to food and it'll want feeding all the time.''

Across the fire the piebald threw the remains of his food into the flames. "Swill," he shouted. "Stinking swill!"

Arn caught Dumarest by the arm. "Leave him."

"He threw away food. There are people out there hungry, watching." Dumarest gestured to the ringing dark. Shapes moved indistinctly in the dusk. "Watching," he said again. "You know what a thing like that does to a hungry man?"

"Sure," admitted the hunter. "It can blow their fuse. Send them in here with rocks and knives. But why should you worry? You look as if you can take care of yourself." He looked past Dumarest to where firelight gleamed on a strand of vagrant hair. "The girl," he said. "You're afraid for her. A rock in the face, a knife, the kick of a boot. I know how it is. But I figure that she can look after things if she has to."

"Perhaps," said Dumarest. "But I'd rather she didn't have to."

Philo yelled again as he flung down his bowl. "Do you know what they're eating up in the barracks now? This very minute? Steak! Eggs! Fried chicken! Braised warbill and roast yalmas! Good food. Real food. Stuff you can get your teeth into and taste."

"Shut up," said a man across the fire.

The piebald sprang to his feet, snarling. His eyes were bloodshot, wild. "You! You want to make me?" He glared, body crouched, hands slightly extended. "You wanna shut my mouth, you come and do it."

"You don't have to keep talking about what we're missing," protested the man.

"That's right," said another. "You want it, you go and get it." He cried out as the piebald sprang across the circle toward him. A boot lashed out and he fell moaning, blood running from his broken mouth.

The piebald strutted around the clearing, eyes like those of an animal. "Anyone else want to argue? Speak up if you do. Fools!" he sneered. "Living in stinking filth like the dogs that you are!"

"That's enough," said Dumarest.

Philo halted, looked at him, body tense, wary. "You object?"

Arn grabbed Dumarest by the arm. "Don't bother, Earl. There's something coming up that'll stop his nonsense. When they see what—"

Dumarest jerked free his arm as the piebald ran forward. There was a smack as he caught the boot swinging toward his face. He gripped, twisted, threw it away as the piebald screamed and spun in order to save his hip. Rising, he stepped forward in the firelight.

"Earl!" Kalin said. "No, Earl, please—"

He ignored her as the piebald rose to his feet. The man crouched in a fighter's stance, hands slightly extended, the fingers of one touching the wrist of the other. He moved, feet stamping the dust, eyes fastened on Dumarest.

"You shouldn't have done that," he crooned.

"Man, you just shouldn't have done that. I'm
going to teach you a lesson now. And after, well,
that little girl of yours is going to need a man to
look after her. A real man." Teeth shone white
between parted lips. "And you're not going to be
much good for anyone soon."

His fingers twitched and firelight splintered on
polished steel. He surged toward Dumarest, his
left arm extended, the elbow crooked, the edge of
the stiffened palm swinging toward the throat.
His right hand swept back, forward, the six-inch
blade swinging in a vicious arc toward the pit of
the stomach.

He was fast, but he had signaled his intentions
and Dumarest was waiting. He stepped sideways,
moving his left so as to clear the swing of the
chopping palm, his right hand dropping, gripping
the wrist of the hand which held the knife, lifting
it up, using its own momentum to swing the blade
in a semicircle which ended at the piebald's
throat.

The man choked and staggered, blood gushing
from his severed jugular, eyes almost starting
from their sockets as he realized what had happened. "You—" he said. "You—"

Dumarest stepped away to avoid the fountain
of blood. His face was cold, hard, registering
neither pity nor satisfaction. He had killed in
order to prevent dying.

Arn rose, stood beside Dumarest, stared somberly down at the body. "Fast," he said. "I've
never seen anyone move as fast as you did then.
One second you were standing there, the blade

swinging toward your gut, the next Philo is dead.''

"Check his pockets," suggested Dumarest. He leaned forward as Arn whistled. "Something?"

"A pass for the commissary," said the other man thoughtfully. He tapped a slip of plastic against his other hand. "No wonder Philo always looked well-fed. He was working for the company as I suspected. They gave him free food and maybe a bonus for every recruit he talked into wearing the collar. Not that he would have had much luck after tonight.''

"That cure you talked about?"

"Yes." Arn tensed as a whistle shrilled in the darkness. From beyond the village, lights bloomed in a brilliant swathe to beat the night. "This is it," he said. "Let's get over there."

VIII

A MAN WAS being punished when they arrived.
He stood in the center of the lighted area, raised
on a platform so that everyone could see the
ghastly pallor of his face. His eyes looked like holes
punched in snow. The gleam of metal shone from
around his throat—the collar all slaves wore and
which, at the touch of a control, would flood
nerve and brain with searing agony. But that pain
was a private thing, coming close at times to providing amusement in the jerkings and twistings of
protesting flesh: ridiculous contortions without
apparent cause. None of those watching would
smile at what would happen to this man.

The area was thronged with spectators. Slaves
for the most part—the object lesson was for their

benefit—ranked in neat files, their overseers watchful as they stood at the rear. A section had been reserved for the civilians: those from the village, the idle and curious and sadistic, the bored and those who were about to be educated. Incredibly the place had a festive air.

Kalin stared at the focus of the lights. "That man, Earl. What are they going to do to him?"

"They're punishing him," he said shortly. "He's up there suffering at this very moment. Not physically," he admitted, "but mentally because he knows what is going to happen to him." He squeezed her arm. "Don't try to look ahead," he warned.

"I won't." She stood on tiptoe, craning, eager to see what was going on. "Why are we here, Earl?"

"Arn wants to show everyone what can happen to those who wear the collar," said Earl. "Counter-propaganda to beat Philo's suggestions."

"I see." She nodded, understanding. "That man," she said. "The one standing there waiting to be punished. What did he do?"

A stooped scavenger from the village who was standing nearby turned and stared at her. "He was smart," he said bitterly. "He tried to help a friend. Someone who wanted to run out on his contract. He figured out a way to remove the collar without blowing the charge. His friend reported him for the sake of immediate freedom and a Low passage on the first ship." He spat. "Some friend!"

Kalin frowned. "Charge?"

"The collars can only be unlocked with a key," said Dumarest. He resisted the impulse to finger his throat. "The band contains an explosive. Break the collar or open it in any way other than with the key and the charge detonates. It will blow the head off the wearer and the hands off anyone touching it."

"How do you know?" she said.

"I know."

"For certain? Have you worn a collar?"

"Once," he said tightly. "On Toy. Why do you ask?"

"No real reason," she said. "It's just that on Solis we have serfs who wear collars. But they aren't loaded with explosives. They are just for identification purposes so that people will know to whom they are bonded."

"Solis sounds a nice place," he said. "Primitive, but nice. I hope it stays that way. No one who has never tried it should think of forcing a man to wear a bomb around his neck."

He lifted his head to watch the poor devil on the platform. Speakers echoed with a studied account of what he had done to deserve this punishment. A psychological semanticist had written the statement and, somehow, he made the lonely figure seem dirty and vile and unfit for the company of decent men.

Kalin sucked in her breath. "No," she whispered. "Dear God, not that! No!"

Dumarest dug his fingers into her arm. "Don't scan," he warned. "Don't do it!"

Her scream rose above the calculated pitch of the speakers.

"What's the matter with her?" The scavenger made as if to come forward. "They haven't even started yet."

"She's ill." Dumarest looked at the contorted face, the twisted mouth. Damn the girl for being curious! "Something she ate," he said. "Poison. I've got to get her to a doctor."

Faces turned, ringing them like watchful discs pricked with curious eyes. Her screams tore at nerve and stomach. Dumarest clamped his hand over her mouth, scooped her from the dirt and, cradling her in his arms, thrust his way toward the edge of the watchers. Overseers stared coldly as they passed. The echo of pounding feet brought Arn panting alongside.

"They don't like you leaving the show," he said, jerking his head at the cloaked figures. "You don't have to come if you're free, but once you do, they reckon you should see it out." He sucked in his cheeks. "Me too," he added. "I want everyone to realize just what being a slave means."

"I'm convinced," said Dumarest curtly. He lowered his hand from Kalin's face and looked into her eyes. "Are you all right now?"

She flushed. "I'm sorry, Earl. It's just that—"

"Forget it," he said quickly. "Don't think about it. Find something else to do." He frowned, thinking. What? What? "Crin," he said. "The man with the broken back. Where is he?"

Arn jerked his head. "Back at Lowtown. His

brothers are looking after him. Haran and Wisar. Why?''

Dumarest paused. The girl needed something to take her mind off what was going to happen beneath the lights. Was happening as far as she was concerned. Despite her promises she would continue to scan the event, like a finger unable to resist touching a sore. To nurse the sick man would be to raise a defense—unless she replaced one horror with another.

"We'll go and see him,'' decided Dumarest. "We might be of some use.''

Nothing could be worse than what was about to happen to the unfortunate slave.

Crin lived with his two brothers in a sagging shack set against a mound of time-settled rubbish. The walls and roof were of fragments: fiberboard, plastic, sheets of protective wrapping. One side was open, a dirty length of material serving to close the entrance against storm or intruders. It was a slum set in reeking dirt with rags for beds and a guttering flame for illumination. The candle was made of grease poured into a tin around a wick of twisted rag.

Beneath it Crin lay supine, reflected light dancing in his open eyes, his lips parted as if he were smiling. Wisar squatted beside him, his voice a soft drone.

". . . and there's a field reaching down to the river, all green with soft grass and dotted with little yellow flowers. You're running over the grass and heading toward the river. Jennie is waiting down there. She's got on her best green slip and her legs and feet are bare. You're going to go swimming together, but not yet. First you have to make betrothal chains for each other from the yellow flowers. You run along, side by side, and each time one of you picks a flower you call out the other's name. Can you hear them? Jennie . . . Crin . . . Jennie . . . Crin . . . Jennie . . . Crin . . .''

Dumarest looked at Haran. "What goes on?"

"We had a monk come in," said Haran. He looked tired, his eyes red and face strained with anxiety. "Crin was a regular attendant at the church, thank God. That meant he was quickly susceptible to hypnotic suggestion. Brother Vesta managed to ease his pain and throw him into a light trance. Now Wisar's feeding him stimulus suggestions. Building up a synthetic life so as to fill his dream world." He knotted his big hands, looked down at his fists. "It makes you feel so damned helpless," he said. "Your own brother, lying there with a ruined spine and there's nothing you can do. Not a damn thing!"

"What's the verdict?" Arn came pushing his way into the shack. "What did the monk say?" From the outside he'd heard every word.

"The spine's gone," said Haran tiredly. "He needs a section transplant before he can walk again. But it's worse than that. Unless he gets some sort of treatment soon he'll die."

"Treatment?" Arn frowned. "What treatment?"

"One of the barbs managed to break the skin and introduce infection." Haran lifted his hands in helpless anger. "I told him to wrap up well! To make sure his padding was secure! The damn fool just wouldn't listen!" He sagged, deflated. "It doesn't matter now. Unless he gets curative therapy he'll be dead within a week."

Kalin made a choked sound deep in her throat. She stood just within the opening, the dancing flame casting shadows on her face. Her eyes were wide as she looked at the sick man.

"Pain," she said. "Pain."

Haran nodded. "The infection is attacking the nerves. Not even hypnosis can help much once it gets a real hold. Nothing can, aside from the specific antidote. Unless he gets it he'll suffer just as much if he'd been slowly lowered into boiling oil." He took a deep breath. "But he won't suffer. I'll see to that."

"You're going to pass him out?" Arn nodded. "It's the best thing you can do. You should—"

"Shut up!" Haran glared, eyes bulging. "You think I'm going to kill him? My own brother! What kind of animal are you?"

"Steady," said Dumarest. "He meant well."

"Like he did out on the hunt? When Crin was smashed down?" Specks of froth showed at the corners of Haran's mouth. "He wanted to kill him then. Kill him as if he'd been an injured dog. Thank God, Wisar and I were there to stop him!"

"All right," soothed Dumarest. The man was almost hysterical with rage and fear. "No one is going to hurt him. What do you intend to do?"

"Have we any choice?" Wisar rose from where he squatted beside the sick man. "We've got to get him medical help. To pay for it one or both of us will have to sell ourselves to the company. Wear the collar,'' he added. ''Become slaves.''

''You're crazy!'' Arn was incredulous. ''You can't mean it. Do you know what happened out near the village tonight? What is still happening? A man is slowly being tortured to death because he broke the rules. Because he wears a collar. Do you really want to throw away your freedom?''

Haran was bitter. ''What freedom? The freedom to watch my brother die in agony? If he wasn't infected I'd be willing to wait. To hope to find a zerd or raise the money in some other way. But we can't wait. If we're to save him we've got to act now. There's nothing else to do.''

''Earl,'' whispered Kalin. ''Is he right?''

Dumarest shook his head. The logical thing was to let the sick man die. Give him an easy passing and make a quick end. But the brothers weren't logical. They were fanatical in regard to their family ties, more than fanatical. Dumarest wondered what held them so close, why they had ever left home.

''We've got to help them, Earl,'' said Kalin softly. ''We can't let them sell themselves.''

He was blunt. ''Why not? What are they to us?''

''Earl!'' Her voice faltered. ''Earl!''

He gripped her arm and led her outside, away from the shack, the air of sickness and defeat. Behind them the candle guttered, throwing odd configurations on the translucent material of the roof and walls. Overhead the stars glittered, coldly hostile in the now solidly black curve of the sky. From the assembly area beyond the village a faint wind blew: chill, numbing, seeming to carry the echoes of ghastly screams.

"You've worn a collar, Earl," she said before he could speak. "You know what it's like."

He waited.

"I can see him, Earl," she whispered. "Faint but getting stronger. You cannot imagine how he is going to suffer if left without help."

"But he isn't going to be left, is he?" Dumarest was bitter. "You know that because you can see just what is going to happen. Well, tell me. What does the clear picture say? The one that really shows the future?"

She gripped his arm, looked up into his face, her eyes filled with dancing lights from the guttering candle.

"I love you, Earl. I want you to do this. Not because I tell you that it is inevitable but because you want to do it for me. For me, Earl. Please!"

"All right," he said heavily. "For you."

And felt the wonderful softness of her lips pressed against his own.

The monk stood beside the door leading into the main entertainment center on Chron. Pete's Bar was enjoying the reaction of men who have watched pain and suffering, agony and death, and were celebrating the fact that they were still alive, still able to enjoy themselves.

"Alms, brother."

Dumarest halted, the girl at his side. He peered into the cowl which shadowed Brother Vesta's thin features. Light from the buildings opposite lit the hollow cheeks, the gentle eyes. From Pete's came a burst of song, the rattle of glasses and the stamping of many feet. A woman laughed, high, shrill. A second joined her, a third.

"Be charitable, brother," said the monk quietly. "Tonight there are those who will die unless they are given warmth and food."

"I know," said Dumarest. "I could be one of them."

"You jest, brother?" The monk looked at the pair. "You both seem to lack nothing."

"Appearances are deceptive, Brother," said Dumarest drily. "We have clothes but nothing else." He looked past the monks toward the building. "I need a stake," he said. "Money with which to make a wager. Will you trust me, Brother?"

"We promise to repay," said Kalin. She was warm beneath her cloak, her helmet. Impatiently she removed it and let the chill night wind blow through the flaming mane of her hair. Reflections made green shimmering pools of her eyes, the light glowed from her translucent skin. "You can keep my helmet if you like," she suggested. "My cloak. I don't need them."

"You will," said the monk quietly. "On Chron the nights grow bitter as winter nears."

"And in the winter?"

"Without such protection you could easily freeze." His eyes burned from the shadow of his cowl. "Your companion could explain more easily than I."

"Stranded travelers have little fat," said Dumarest evenly. "Traveling Low keeps them thin. Without body-fat to act as insulation the cold bites deep. But we are lucky. We have both been traveling High." He looked at the monk. "I was not jesting when I asked for a stake," he said quietly. "I will return it ten times over. A good investment, Brother."

The monk hesitated, his eyes on the girl's hair. The wind pressed the cowl tight against his cheek as he turned to look at Dumarest. "Your name, brother?"

Dumarest told him. The girl added. "And I am Kalin of Solis. Will you keep my helmet and cloak?"

"No," said the monk. His hand slipped within his sleeve, returned bearing coins. "Here, brother." He handed them to Dumarest. "Good fortune."

A man checked them as they entered the warmth of the bar, eyes hard as he looked for signs of poverty or desperation. They displayed neither. Retaining her outer garments so as to hide the rough tunic beneath, Kalin followed Dumarest to the gaming tables where men clustered around a wheel and dancing ball. The minimum stake was too large for their resources.

"Drinks, sir and madam?" A waiter sidled to stand before them. Dumarest shook his head.

"Not yet. I am looking for a game I find amusing. Highest, lowest, man-in-between. Always before drinking, I consult the Goddess of Luck.''

The waiter understood; gamblers were superstitious. ''Over to the left, sir. In the far corner.'' He followed them with his eyes, wondering why the woman should wear cloak and helmet in the warmth of the bar. He shrugged. Women, who could predict them? But, even so, it was odd.

''The waiter is suspicious,'' said Dumarest as they crossed the floor. ''He is watching us. We must act quickly.'' He reached the table and stood looking at the cards. The dealer shuffled, cut, stacked and cut the deck into three.

Kalin touched her forehead as if easing an irritation.

''Center stack,'' said Dumarest. He put down all his money. ''Match or set stake?''

''I'll match it,'' said a man. He set money on the left-hand stack. Another took the right. Dumarest won.

Again the dealer shuffled and cut. Employed by the house, he took little interest in the game which was run mostly as a sop to those with little money and limited imagination. Kalin touched the helmet above her left ear.

Dumarest backed the winning deck.

And again.

The fourth time he picked up his winnings he shook his head. ''This isn't going to last,'' he said. ''I've got a feeling.''

Kalin yawned, moved casually away, stared at a pair of bouncing dice.

Dumarest lost. And won. Then lost again.

He left the table, looked for the waiter and found him staring with interest at the girl. Ordering drinks, Dumarest joined her where she watched a man trying to match a previous throw.

"Give me some money, darling," she said. "All of it that he makes his point the hard way," she said. The dice rolled, settled, showed a pair of threes.

"The lady wins!" The stickman checked her bet and pushed over coins.

Dumarest shook his head as she gave it to him. "You keep it. You seem lucky tonight."

He followed her to the spinning wheel. A rainbow splotched a numbered cloth and colored balls spun in eye-twitching confusion. A bell chimed.

"Bets!" called the spinner.

Coins thudded to the table.

"Red, green, blue, four, six, nine," panted a man. He was the kind of gambler the bar loved, backing an impossible combination in the hope of winning astronomical odds.

Kalin shook her head. "No," she decided. "I can't make up my mind fast enough. I guess I don't know the combinations as well as I should." They moved on to another wheel, a ball, nine compartments. "This is better."

The odds were lower but the chances of winning greater, and accumulating at five to one she quickly hit the limit. Hit, stayed for a few spins, then deliberately lost a time or two.

Dumarest ordered more drinks.

"The lady seems lucky tonight, sir," said the

waiter. "I have been watching. Good fortune attends her."

"And myself." Dumarest turned to look at where a touch of red glowed above a cloak striped in green and yellow. As he watched she impatiently removed the helmet.

The waiter made a sound of appreciation. "Such hair!"

"As soft as silk to the touch," said Dumarest. His voice held a leer. "A strange prize to find on such a world. That is why I claim myself fortunate."

He moved away and watched as Kalin won more money. Casually he turned, eyes moving over the rim of his glass as he sipped his drink. Lowering it, his elbow collided with the girl, the contents of the glass dashing over his clothes.

"Out," he said as she stooped to help him wipe away the sticky fluid. "Lose a couple of times, try another table and lose again. Small amounts but steady. Win once and then quit."

"But, Earl we can't go wrong!"

"You've attracted attention. The house-men are watching. Get out before they guess you are a sensitive."

Outside with a wind blowing cold down the street she said, "We could have won a lot more, Earl."

"You're greedy," he said. "We did well. Be satisfied that they assumed you had a lucky streak. If nothing else, we've retained the opportunity to try again." Halting before the impassive figure of the monk, Dumarest poured coins into the bowl he carried for the collection of alms. It was a score the amount that he had borrowed. "My thanks to you, Brother. We were fortunate."

Brother Vesta looked at the money, at the man and at the girl. "You are generous, brother. Many will have reason to be thankful."

His eyes were brooding as he stared after the couple as they walked down the street.

IX

BERTRAM ARSINI, the mad artist from Xoltan, had built the statue and, finding it unsatisfactory, had put out his eyes and ears so that he might no longer be tormented by the sight and sound of unattainable beauty. The High Monk of the time had not been so critical. He had ordered the statue to be placed in an appropriate setting and now, a millennium later, the work had yet to be equaled.

Brother Jerome paused, looking up at the magnificent representative of the human spirit. A woman, the external mother, stood on a ball of writhing flame. Her face was upraised, her hands lifted, her body a composite of the ten most beautiful women of the artist's era. She was youth and beauty and mature understanding. The girl with whom to play at love, the mother to whom to turn, the goddess to worship.

A thousand shades of pigment stained the crystal of the hundred-foot construction. Ten thousand components filled the solid-state interior. Radiation powered the electronic devices which kept the surface clean, bright and shining. At night it glowed with a warm, inner light. At certain periods the crystalline fabrication distorted, producing pizeo-electric signals causing the entire fabrication to vibrate in abstract, entrancing melody of pure tonal sequences.

A time-bell chimed from over the gardens and the High Monk continued on his way. Past ponds filled with luminescent fish, flowers of a dozen planets, bushes bearing succulent fruits. The gardens of Hope were as famous as the statue.

Brother Fran met him as he made his way toward the building. The secretary fell into step beside his superior, hands clasped within the wide sleeves of his robe, head bent as he apparently studied the intricate mosaics of the path.

Jerome sighed. Brother Fran had a way of communicating without words. "You have something to tell me," he said. "What is it?"

"I do not wish to interrupt your meditation, Brother."

"I wasn't meditating," said Jerome. "I was simply walking and dreaming of the past and of things to come. That statue, for example. Has it ever occurred to you that perhaps it holds a deeper significance than we realize? The woman could be representing not the eternal mother but the human race itself. The human race bursting free from the planet of its origin to reach out and touch the stars. To touch them and settle on them and to spread and grow.''

"An old legend,'' said Brother Fran quietly. "In Arsini's time it was, perhaps, a little stronger than it is now. But I do not think that he intended any such thing. He was an artist but he was also a mathematician and a man of logic. I find it hard to believe that he could have ever taken such a legend seriously.''

"Because of logic?''

"Yes. After all, how could it ever have been possible for all the members of the human race ever to have originated on one small world? They breed, true, but the diversity of types, the skin-coloring and racial characteristics—'' He shook his head. "If the legend is true, it must have been a very strange world, Brother.

"Perhaps.'' Jerome didn't care to press the point. "My hour of relaxation over,'' he reminded. "What do you wish to tell me?''

"We have news of the girl.''

"The one Centon Frenchi claims is his daughter?''

"That is the one. She is on Chron.''

Jerome frowned, looking at the mosaics but not seeing them, his mind busy with speculation.

"There can be no doubt as to the identification,'' continued the secretary. "She gave her name as Kalin of Solis. I checked her physical characteristics with the biometer and her coloring substantiates her claim. Only on Solis do they have such a peculiar shade of hair. They breed for it. It is unique to the planet.''

"You go too fast, Brother," said Jerome
mildly. "A girl who apparently originated on
Solis is on Chron. She, also apparently, matched
the identification given us by Centon Frenchi of
Sard. There appears to be an inconsistency. If she
was born on Solis how can she be the girl Frenchi
is seeking?''

"Her maternal grandmother came from Solis,"
said Fran evenly. "We have already discussed
the possibility of her being an atavist. As for the
rest, her name and planet, she could easily have
lied.''

Jerome frowned. He must be getting old to
overlook the obvious, but there were so many details, so many things to bear in mind, so many decisions to make.

"I have prepared a message for Centon Frenchi," said the secretary. "Informing him of what
we have discovered. With your permission I shall
send it.''

"Not yet." The High Monk looked up at the
sky, at the statue, as a ripple of music sighed in
crystalline perfection. "There seems to be no
need for undue haste. Is the girl alone?''

"There is a man with her. Earl Dumarest. Our
information on him is favorable, though he does
not belong to the Church. He appears to have
reason to hate the Cyclan.''

"The Cyclan," murmured Jerome. "I wonder
if—?''

Brother Fran was impatient. "You still do not

trust Centon Frenchi, Brother? I fail to see your reason."

"Perhaps I have none," admitted the High Monk. "I could even be mistaken—what human is infallible? But there is no need for haste. And I think," he added, "that we should know a little more than we do."

"About the girl?"

"No, Brother," said Jerome quietly. "About Solis."

Kramm slammed his hand down on the table with force enough to make the goblets jump from the boards. "How long?" he demanded. "How long must we wait before the cyber tells us just what to do in order to reverse the downward swing of our fortunes?"

Komis poured a little wine, sipped, stared thoughtfully into the glass. His brother was impatient, but not wholly without cause. Mede seemed to be working on some devious plan of his own. He had taken long journeys up and down the coast, visiting other farms and establishments, sectioning the area and gathering an apparently unrelated mass of data. Yet who could tell how the cyber went about his work?

Beer gurgled as Kramm manipulated the jug. Only he and the Master of Klieg remained at the table; the others had long since gone to their rooms. Outside a wind gusted from the sea, cold, a harbinger of coming winter. Within the great hall a fire leaped from an open grate. Kramm's goblet made a rapping noise as he set it on the polished wood.

"He was right about one thing," he said gloomily. "The thren are getting out of hand. Fifteen mares within a week. I've had the men clear the more distant pastures and concentrate the herd. I thought we should double the beak bounty," he added. "It might make the men a little more eager to make a kill."

"I agree—but only if they are willing to pay for their cartridges," said Komis. "The fire rate per kill is already too high. Double the bounty and it will get higher." He smiled a little. "Not everyone is as good a shot as you, my brother."

"And they will take wild chances," admitted Kramm. "Fill the air with lead and hope a thren runs into a bullet." His hands tightened into fists. "What we need is a flier loaded with dust. The cyber was right in that if in nothing else."

"A cyber is never wrong." Komis rose, walked down the hall to stand before the dancing colors of the fire. Kramm joined him, thicker-set, younger, a pea from a similar pod. Their faces glowed with colored shadows. "Tomorrow I want to ride out and select the best of our beasts. Reduce down to one third of our present holding. Save the breeding stock, naturally, but the rest must go for sale."

The inhalation of Kramm's breath merged with the hiss of unburned gases from a crack in one of the logs. "Are you serious?"

"I am."

"Is this the cyber's plan?" Kramm turned from

the fire, eyes greenly surveying the empty hall.
"Where is he anyway? Back or off on one of his
journeys?"

"In his room or somewhere about the house."
Komis fell into step with his brother as Kramm
paced the length of the hall. "The plan is my own.
If we cannot contain the depredations of the
thren, and the cyber says we cannot, then there is
little point in working to provide food for the
birds. Winter is approaching. That means we
must supply shelter and fodder for the beasts.
The thren will increase their attacks."

"Destroy them," said Kramm bitterly.
"Quickly, before they destroy us."

"How? With radioactives?" Komis shook his
head. "There could be a better way. Professor
Helman at the university is working on a bac-
teriophage which could provide the answer. A
selective strain of mutated disease which will
safely destroy the thren and no other kind of life.
I have promised him the use of a dozen horses for
developing his serums."

"And the cyber?"

Komis looked at his brother. "I do not understand."

"Will he be willing to let you make your own
plans, go your own way?"

"Cyber Mede is a guest," said the Master of
Klieg. "I shall be grateful for any help he is
pleased to offer, any suggestions he may care to
make. But there is only one master of this place
and it is not the cyber."

Kramm blew out his cheeks. "I wanted to hear

you say that. But the sale. Is it wise? Prices now are not at their best."

"A living animal will fetch more than a dead one," said Komis evenly. "And we need the money. We need all the money we can get."

"For Keelan?"

"Who else?"

Komis turned from his brother and left the hall. A passage led to his study, the book-lined room where he conducted the affairs of the estate. Here were the records and rolls, the genealogical charts, the breeding details traversing past generations of both animals and men. A radio vision communicator stood against a wall, incongruous against the rough stone, the woven drapes, but normal enough on this world where everything which could be made by hand was so constructed. Economy dictated the houses, the furnishings, the very clothing the people wore; necessity the radiovision communicator, the electric lighting, the availability of a flier.

Files lay open on the desk, their neat figures telling a too familiar story. And yet how could they economize? How?

Retrenchment wasn't enough, Komis knew. Economies would only stave off the inevitable. Making the resources of a week last ten days would not solve the problem. They needed to earn more, not make do with less.

But, again, how?

Surely the cyber would know.

Komis found him in the place with the open

side, the patio with pillars facing onto the sea, the open area filled with the hum and drone of the wind, the scent and sound of the ocean as it tore at the rocks below.

Lights shone from the rooms behind, the one where the attendant sat, the one from which Komis emerged. He stood, looking at the night, then saw a shifting gleam of scarlet, the glitter of the Cyclan seal emblazoned on the cyber's robe. Mede's cowl shadowed his face so that only the scarlet was visible, a red shadow against the dark of the sky. Then he moved and the light turned him into a living flame.

"My lord?"

"I was looking for you," said Komis. He stepped forward and the door closed behind him cutting off most of the light. "I did not expect to find you here."

"Is it forbidden? I did not know, my lord. I followed a stair to the sound of the sea. But if this part of your house is reserved for the family, then I shall leave immediately." Mede hesitated. "With your permission, my lord."

"Stay." There was no point in the cyber leaving now. "You have made many investigations," said Komis directly. The time for delicacy was past. "I must ask if you have arrived at a decision."

Mede was precise. "I make no decisions, my lord. I advise, nothing more."

"And?"

"My lord?"

Komis was impatient. "Must we play with

words? What do you advise me to do? How can I
increase the fortune of Klieg?''

"I think you misunderstand my purpose here,
my lord.'' Mede's voice was a modulated accompaniment to the gusting wind. "I cannot tell you
what to do. I can only advise you as to the course
of any action you may choose to take. However I
appreciate your concern, my lord. It cannot be
easy for you to accept the fact that your people
face inevitable ruin.''

Komis turned, saw a bench, sat on the cold
stone. "Are you trying to frighten me, cyber?''

"For what purpose, my lord?'' In the shadow
of his cowl, Mede's shaven skull was a glimmer-
ing blur. Thin hands tucked themselves into wide
sleeves as the wind tugged at the scarlet fabric of
his robe. "In all matters the Cyclan remains neutral. I am a servant of the Cyclan.''

"And so you also remain neutral.'' Komis
drew a deep breath. "Tell me,'' he commanded.
"I must know the worst.''

"The income of your estate is limited,'' said
Mede smoothly. "I have already warned of the
result to be expected from the depredations of the
thren. But it is more than that. I have studied the
figures, the land, the markets for the past twenty
years. Your people and dependents increase but
your resources do not. Even so, you would have
managed on a gradually sliding curve until the
position had been breached where you would
solve the problem by the use of other
technologies. However, a short while ago something happened which accelerated the curve.

Your outgoings increased to the limit of income and beyond. You spent from capital, my lord. You entered into debt.''

Komis moved restlessly on the bench.

"Your situation was delicate to begin with," continued the cyber. "It was as if your economy were balanced on the edge of a knife. A little push to one side and it would fall. You gave it that push, my lord.''

"I spent money," admitted Komis. "I borrowed money. But we have stock and land and men to work the land. How can you talk of ruin?''

"A word with relative meanings," admitted the cyber. "Ruin to one could be fortune to another. But for you, my lord, it means retrenchment, the loss of those who now give you loyalty, the sale of land and the loss of certain expensive services you now enjoy.''

Komis saw the movement of his eyes, the glitter as light from the room reflected from the pupils. "My sister.''

"My lord?''

Komis rose, tall, hard. "You are talking of my sister when you talk of 'expensive services.' The physicians to attend her, the life-support apparatus, the research to find a path to guide her back to health." And before that there had been the endless stream of doctors, the time bought at the big medical computers, the tests and treatments, the hope and disappointments, and, always, the expense, the expense. But what was the value of a sister's life?

Mede bowed. "I understand, my lord.''

"Do you, cyber? I wonder if you can? If you are able?" Komis shook his head. The man was a guest! "I am sorry. Some things disturb me and I speak without thinking. My sister has been ill for many years. She was, is, greatly loved."

"With your permission, my lord, I would like to see her. We of the Cyclan are versed in medical matters."

"Are you a doctor?"

"No, my lord, but if I knew the full nature of her ailment it is barely possible that I could suggest some helpful therapy."

Komis hesitated. Keelan was not to be exposed to the eyes of the curious and yet Mede could possibly be of use. His mind did not work in the same way as other men's and he belonged to an organization which spanned the galaxy. Cybers were to be found at every center of rule and learning. Perhaps—?

He shook his head. Tomorrow, he would think about it, but not now. Now the cyber would have to wait. As Keelan had waited. As she was still waiting. Tomorrow was soon enough.

From his window Mede could see the roofs of the out-buildings, the top of the surrounding wall, the rolling scrub of the downs beyond. To one side the path curved as it fell into the valley, invisible now as were the downs and the wall, shielded in the clouded night. Only the roofs of the outhouses reflected the gleam from his window, the shifting glow of the signal torch burning high above the gate.

Carefully he drew the curtains, the thick weave proof against a prying eye. The door was fastened with a wooden bar which slid in wooden sockets. Thick, crude, but both simple to make and effective for its purpose. He engaged it and touched the bracelet locked about his left wrist. Invisible forces flowed from the instrument and built a barrier against any electronic device being able to focus in his vicinity. His privacy assured, Mede turned to the bed and lay supine on the warm coverings. Above his eyes the roof bore paintings of animals and the details of a hunt.

Barbarism, he thought. When men lived close to the soil they seemed to share the attributes of the animals they tended or slaughtered for food—forgetting the fined instruments of their brains in the urges of the flesh. It was a mistake no cyber could ever make.

Relaxing, he closed his eyes and concentrated on the Samatchazi formula. Gradually he lost the senses of taste, smell, touch and hearing. Had he opened his eyes he would have been blind. Divorced of external stimuli his brain ceased to be irritated, gained tranquility and calm, became a thing of pure intellect, its reasoning awareness the only thread with normal existence. Only then did the grafted Homochon elements become active. Rapport was almost immediate.

Mede expanded with vibrant life.

No two cybers had the same experience. For Mede it was as if he walked over a field resplendent with flowers and each flower was the shining light of truth. His feet sank into the field so that he

was a part of it, sharing the same massed and intertwining roots of the flowers, intermeshed inex-
tricably with the filaments which stretched across
the universe to infinity. He saw it and was a part
of it, as it was a part of him. The flowers were part
of a living organism which filled the galaxy and he
also was a similar flower.

And, at the heart of the system, a swelling node
in the complex of interengaged minds, was the
headquarters of the Cyclan. Buried deep beneath
miles of rock on a lonely planet, the central intelligence absorbed his knowledge as a sponge
would absorb water from a pool of dew. There
was no verbal communication—only mental
communion, quick, almost instantaneous organic
transmission against which even ultra-radio was
the merest crawl.

*"Your area the one with the highest index of
probability. Concentrate on determination of true
data to the exclusion of all else. Speed is of the
utmost urgency."*

Mede framed a suggestion. *"Isolating of time
factor could have high relevancy. Cross-checking
with medical facilities in area could confirm prediction."*

*"Confirmation will follow. Immediate action is
to determine probability and to take full action to
safeguard as previously instructed. Emphasize
the necessity for speed. On no account will failure
be tolerated. Matter most important."*

That was all.

The rest was pure, mental intoxication.

Always, after rapport had been broken, was

this period when the Homochon elements sank into quiescence and the machinery of the body began to realign itself with mental control. Mede hovered in a dark nothingness, a pure intelligence untrammeled by the limitations of the body, sensing strange memories and unexperienced situations. Shards and scraps of mental overflow from other intelligences. The idle discard from other minds. It was the overflow power of central intelligence, the radiated thoughts of the tremendous cybernetic complex which was the heart of the Cyclan.

One day, if he proved himself, he would become a living part of that gigantic intelligence. His body would age and his senses dull but his brain would remain as active as ever. Then the technicians would take him, remove his brain, fit it into a vat of nutrient fluids and attach the tubes and instruments of a life-support apparatus. He would join the others, his brain hooked in series with the rest.

He would be a part of, and yet the whole of, a complex of a vast number of brains. An organic computer working continuously to solve the secrets of the universe.

An intelligence against which there could be no resistance.

X

ON CHRON, WINTER was a tiger, lurking, dangerous. The winds came blustering down from the
icy mountains, harsh and loaded with the chemical fumes released from the fused magma of the
mines. The sleet held acid which burned unpro-
tected skin and caused painful rashes and sores.
Food grew even more scarce, as did fuel. Men
huddled around the smelters, risking asphyxia-
tion for the sake of warmth, almost hoping to be
caught by the rare patrols of company guards—
for, enslaved, they would be fed.

Dumarest grew leaner, harder as he scoured
the countryside; then one morning Kalin woke
screaming.

"Steady!" Dumarest moved quickly to her
side. He wore a thick cloak and his body was

huge by reason of the rags bound about his body over his normal clothing. "It's all right," he soothed. "There's nothing to worry about."

"Earl!" She clung to him. "Earl, don't go!"

Gently he disengaged her arms from around his neck. A metered fire stood against the wall. He fed coins into the slot and threw the switch. Beam heat warmed the bed, the area around it. A hotplate provided heat to boil coffee. Through the window shone the false light of early dawn.

He waited until the coffee had boiled, added sugar, handed the girl a cup and took one himself. "We went through all this last night," he said. "I've got to go out again with Arn and the others. You know why."

"No," she protested. "I don't know why." She sat upright in bed, her hair a glowing waterfall in the red warmth of the fire. Traveler-fashion, she was fully dressed against the cold, against thieves and the possible need to get up and run. Here in this hotel room there was no real need for such caution but Dumarest didn't object.

She might, he thought bleakly, have need of such teaching later on.

He sipped his coffee and sat enjoying the taste and warmth. Soon enough he would be where both were almost unobtainable. "Kalin," he said. "You promised me not to look ahead."

She was stubborn. "I agreed, I didn't promise. And why shouldn't I see what is going to happen?"

"Because it makes you wake screaming," he said quietly. "Because you can't be sure of what you see." He sipped again, staring at her over the edge of the cup. "What did you see?"

"Pain," she said. "And blood. And you all hurt."

"But you can't tell exactly when," he said. "Or where. Or how. That is why I ask you not to look. Not to attempt to scan our futures. Some things we don't need to know. Some things, knowing, we cannot avoid. I don't want to go out on a hunt knowing that I'm going to be hurt. The mere fact of knowing could make it certain." It was getting too involved. He swallowed the last of his coffee and put away the cup. "I'd better get moving. The others will be waiting."

"Let them wait." Woman-like, she was indifferent to the comfort of others when a problem filled her mind. "Why, Earl?" she insisted. "Why do you have to go out at all? We can make enough money at the gambling tables to live in relative comfort. We could make enough to buy us passage away from here. Why can't we just do that?"

Dumarest was cold. "You're talking like a fool and you know it. They suspect you're a sensitive and only tolerate us playing because we've enough sense to be content with small winnings and because we make a good advertisement. If we went out for a killing you'd find they'd bar our bets. If we managed to force them to pay they would have men waiting for us outside. Knowing what's going to happen doesn't always mean you can avoid it. Chron is a small place as far as we're concerned. We couldn't hope to hide."

He smiled at her taut face, brushed the tips of his fingers over her white cheek.

"Look," he said. "Let's be sensible. You've got money, somewhere safe to live, heat and food when you want it. Gambling has provided that, and with luck, will continue to provide it."

"Then why go out?" she said again. "Why risk your life? You could wind up like Crin. Lying helpless with a broken back. You don't have to help his brothers find money for a healing operation." She clung to him. "Earl! Don't go! You don't have to!"

He gripped her arms. "I do."

"But why? Why?"

"Because we're in a trap!" He moved his grip to her wrists and caught the scent of her hair as he pulled free of her arms. "We're stranded, girl, can't you understand? There's no free work here, no way to earn enough money to buy a passage. We could steal it, but the company uses scrip, has guards and checks the field. We can't win it—not with you suspected of being a sensitive. So we have to make it. What other way is there than by hunting a zardle and hoping to find a zerd?"

She was stubborn. "A Low passage wouldn't cost all that much."

"Sure," he admitted. "If I wore the collar for a year, didn't spend a penny of my pay, didn't gamble or drink or run up any bills for food or clothing I might just about manage it. Of course there would be the interest charges on the money I'd borrowed but a second year should take care of that." He leaned toward her, smiling. "Will you wait for me, Kalin?"

"Forever, Earl." Her eyes met his and he knew that she wasn't joking. "I'd wait until the sun went out."

"I wouldn't let you." He rose, huge in the warm glow of the fire, almost shapeless because of the padding. "I couldn't be without you that long."

"Thank you, darling, for saying that."

"I mean it." He stooped, kissed her, tasted the heaven of her lips. "Don't worry," he said quietly. "I'll get you out of here."

Then he was gone and she sat alone in the bed, seeing a succession of images, pictures of the future. She fought the screams which, born of fear, rose in futile negation.

Arn shuffled his feet in the freezing dust. "You're late," he said.

"So I'm late." Dumarest looked over the assembled knot of men. "Have you got the nets? The other stuff?"

"It's all here."

Dumarest checked the group. Arn, Haran and his brother Wisar, five others—a total of nine. Too many, perhaps. Three men with lasers would have been more efficient: one to tend camp, one to cover and one to hunt. But three men wouldn't have been able to transport the meat—they would have killed for fun, not food.

As the company officials did during the fine weather. Killing for the sake of it, hoping to be rewarded with a zerd but rarely finding any. Dumarest thought he knew why.

"All right," he said, lifting his voice. "Before

we start let's get a couple of things straight. Kalin has supplied the nets and supplies so she gets two shares. Arn, Haran and Wisar know the prey and terrain so they get a share and a half. I get the same. Any objections?"

A man coughed. "That applies to everything? Head, skin and tails?"

"Everything," said Dumarest. "Including any zerds we may find. Kalin gets a double share. Agreed?"

Breath plumed in white vapor as they nodded.

"The other thing is that I'm in full charge," said Dumarest. "What I say goes. If you don't like it you can walk away now. Try walking away later and I'll cut you down." He looked at their strained faces. "We're not coming back empty-handed on this trip," he said. "We're going to stay out until we get something worth getting. All in favor?"

"Suits me," said a man. The rest added their agreement.

Dumarest nodded to Arn. "Right," he said. "Let's check the padding and start moving."

At first the going was easy, long slopes rising up from the village. The path led between the landing field and the smelter. On the field stood ships; lines of men like ants loading their bellies with metal, trotting to the cracking whips of overseers. Above the smelter shone the red glow of electronic fire, the swirling clouds of released fumes shot with streaks of burning as combustible gases reached flash-point. Well away from both smelter and field, the gaudy bubbles of Hightown shone almost iridescent in the weak light of a late dawn.

Haran looked at them and spat. "Warmth," he said. "Comfort. Running water. Good food and clean clothing. Soft beds and soap and piped music—and my brother is lying in frozen filth!"

"It's the system," said Lough. He was one of the new men and grunted as he shifted the weight of his pack. "Some have and a lot haven't. It's always been the same."

"It always will be," said another morosely. "Like eating, sleeping, getting born, dying. It's a law of nature."

"Like hell it is!" Wisar glowered at the bubbles. "Maybe we should change that law," he said tightly. "Go in there and take a little of what we need and they can't use. When I think of Crin—!"

"How is he?" said Lough. "Still no improvement?"

"There won't be until he gets a section-transplant." Wisar tore his eyes from the bubbles and looked directly ahead. "He can move his head and arms but that's about all. At that he's lucky. If it hadn't been for Earl buying treatment to neutralize the zardle poison he'd have died long ago."

"No, he wouldn't," corrected Haran. "He'd be walking about alive and well—but we'd both be wearing a collar for life." He paused as the track divided. One branch curved to run down into a shallow valley, the other pointed to where mountains loomed in the far distance. "Which way, Arn? Left or right?"

"To the mountains," said Arn, and then as Haran headed right—"Two for one's a bad exchange. The way things are you've all got a chance to get away from here fit and free."

Wisar was bitter. "If we're lucky. If we find a zerd. If it's big enough so that our share will pay for Crin's operation. If we can have money over for three Low passages. That's a lot of 'ifs,' Arn."

"It's half of what Crin would have had to worry about if you'd sold yourselves and he had to buy you free of the collar." Arn looked back at the village, at Lowtown beyond. "How about that? Are they willing to operate without you selling out?"

"Sure," said Haran. "Why not? They set the price and we have to pay it. If we had the cash there would be no problem."

Dumarest could appreciate the unconscious irony. If they had cash none of them would have any problems. He called out as one of the men forged ahead.

"Bernie! Slow down!"

The man halted, waited for the others to come abreast. He was a tall, thin man with a peaked face and anxious eyes. A new arrival impatient to get a stake and be on his way. "Why slow down?" he demanded. "It's cold. Keep moving fast and you get warm."

"You also start to sweat," said Dumarest. "In this weather that can be fatal. You slow down." He explained: "The sweat freezes and you get coated with a film of ice. Hypothermia can kill as surely as a bullet. So just remember not to move so fast that you start to sweat."

"But we want to get there," protested the man. "Get on with the job."

"We'll get there," promised Dumarest. "And when we do you'll have reason to sweat. In the meantime just do as I say. Understand?"

Bernie swallowed. "Sure, Earl," he said. "I understand."

The path veered further to the right, heading to where the giant power piles poured a flood of energy into the mining complex. In the lower regions of the mountains machines gouged holes in the frozen dirt, laid man-thick cables, ripped ducts and vents from the buried ore. Power, created by the tremendous wash of eddy-currents, fused the buried minerals, freed the metal, sent it gushing through the vents into waiting molds.

From the release-ducts columns of lambent gases rose shrieking toward the sky—billowing in a corrosive cloud of searing chemicals. The rising columns caused winds to blow into the area, filling the gap left by the rising mass of heated air. Convection currents sent the great masses of atmosphere swirling, shedding their water content in a clammy mist which clung to the ground like a reeking gas.

In the heat and hell of poisoned fog collared men sweated and coughed and screamed as vagrant gusts drove living steam against wincing flesh.

Others crouched behind protective shields as white-hot metal gushed into molds, splashing searing droplets, or worse, seething in baffled fury behind temporary blockages. When that happened men had to run with long rods to poke and clear away the obstructing mass before the trapped devil behind could erupt into unwanted paths.

Heat and smoke and dazzling fire. Corrosive gases and blistering steam. The ever-present risk of dying beneath a gush of molten metal, of having flesh seared from the bone, of being cooked alive. The place was a living hell. At times the eddy-currents veered—blasting the area with invisible but all-consuming death.

The mines of Chron were not noted for their gentleness.

"Look at it," commanded Dumarest. He stood on the slope of a mountain, facing the swirling mass of gas and vapor, the flaming discharge and incessant lightning of the manmade storm. "Take a good look. That's what we're all trying to avoid."

A man shuffled his feet on the frozen dust. "You don't have to convince us, Earl. We all know what it's all about."

"Out here you do," admitted Dumarest. "But back in Lowtown? I've heard the whispering. Wear a collar and live easy. When you're cold and freezing and half-starved such talk is tempting. Soft beds, good food, medical attention. The easy life." He lifted an arm and pointed toward the mine. "Well, there it is. All of it. Remember it when we're facing a zardle. When you might feel tempted to let go the net, run maybe, decide there are easier ways of getting something to eat." He dropped his arm. "All right," he said. "You've seen it. Now let's get moving."

They marched all through the long, freezing
day, plunging deeper into the heart of the mountains, following narrow, almost invisible trails
made an unguessable time ago. More often than
not there were no trails and Arn led the way cautiously, watching for hidden traps and dangerous
sections. Apparently solid rock yielded to the impact of a boot. As they marched, they snatched up
clumps of the thorny scrub for later use as fuel. As
the sun vanished beneath the horizon Dumarest
called a halt.

"We'll camp here," he decided. "There are
rock walls to reflect the heat of a fire, nothing
hanging above to fall on us, a narrow ledge leading
up to and beyond this point. You and you." He
pointed to two men. "Go a hundred yards down
the trail to each side. Set up a trip wire and an
alarm. Bernie, gather rocks to build a fire. Lough,
you start breaking the scrub into small pieces."

An hour later they sat around the glowing em-
bers of a fire, internally warmed by hot food and
scalding coffee. A wind droned and gusted past the
sheltered spot, lifting little flurries of glowing ash
from the fire.

Arn threw more scrub on the fire, the seared
tissue of his cheek glistening in the leaping brightness. Bernie called from where he sat with his back
against a rock, feet thrust toward the blaze. His
boots were shabby, torn, rags filling the gaps.
"When are we going to get down to work?"

Arn shrugged, looked at Dumarest. "Ask
Earl," he said. "He's the man in charge."

"That's right," said Dumarest. Firelight shone on a circle of faces, reflected from watching eyes. "We're after zerds," he said. "To get them I figure we have to go where they're to be found. Now the normal method of hunting seems to be to go out, find a zardle, hit it and hope. With luck you get the head, skin and tail and some meat besides without losing a man in the process. More often than not, someone gets injured. Now and again you find a zerd. Not often, just enough to keep others using the same system. I think it's wrong.

"It's wrong because the hunters are trusting too much to luck. Luck that they find a zardle at all. Luck that they don't get hurt. Luck that they find a zerd. Usually it's bad luck. There's a reason for it, of course. The nets are on hire. The men are hungry and eager for food. They go out mostly in the summer when there is more plentiful game. Wrong again. The time to hunt is now when the weather is against the beasts. The cold will slow them down and they'll have to stick close to where they can feed. That means they'll be close together."

"Easier for us," said Lough thoughtfully. "I haven't hunted before but you make sense. That right, Arn?"

The scarred man nodded. "That's right. I've figured this all out for myself, but I couldn't get enough cash together to buy supplies to try it. Now we've got supplies, nets, all we need. If we don't get a zerd this trip I'll sell myself to the mines!"

"We'll find them," said Dumarest. "It's a matter of picking the right beasts. Mostly the hunters run into young ones, those driven off the territory of the older males. A zerd takes time to grow. Sometimes the young ones have them, but mostly they don't. I'm betting that the situation is reversed among the older zardles." He put out a hand, stopped Lough from adding more fuel to the fire. "Save it for the morning. We've a heavy day ahead." He raised his voice. "Get some sleep now. I'll stand the first watch. I'll awaken one of you in an hour."

He picked up one of the spears they had brought with them. A scrap length of pipe, six feet long, the end hammered so as to grip a point of glass pressure-flaked to razor point and edge. It was crude but effective: a thrust in a soft region would penetrate and rip as if it had been tempered steel.

Leaning on it, Dumarest stood guard, listening to the gust and sigh of the wind, the faint rattles coming from stones shaking in cans attached to the trip-wires, the heavy breathing and snores of fatigued men.

XI

HE WOKE, RISING through layers of ebon chill, mentally counting seconds as he had done so often when traveling Low. Counting as the drugs took effect, the pulmotor forced his lungs and heart into rhythm, the eddy currents warmed the frozen solidity of his flesh and blood. He almost felt the heady euphoria of resurrection. Then Dumarest opened his eyes.

The fire was a dull ember casting a dim glow over the rocks, the shapes of sleeping men. To one side the guard leaned against a wall, his spear propped close at hand. Dumarest frowned and raised himself on one elbow.

Something rattled in the darkness: the jangle of pebble-loaded cans strung on the trip wire down the trail.

Dumarest sprang to his feet, shouting, "Up! Up, all of you! On guard!"

It came as he stopped to snatch his spear and throw dried twigs on the fire. A head, gaping, fangs gleaming in the rising flicker of firelight, eyes deeply set and redly wicked. Spines crested the sloping skull and scales made a metallic shimmer on the rippling hide.

"A zardle!" said Arn. "A young one—but hungry!"

Eight feet long, two high, it rushed forward on taloned legs, mouth gaping, barbed tail lashing with the bone-snapping fury of a whip. The guard screamed as it smashed him against the rock, screamed again as it whipped across his throat, then fell.

"Haran! Wisar! Get to its side! Lough! Bernie! Get on its back and smash its spine!" Arn swore as the tail lashed at the injured guard. Cloth and padding flew beneath the impact. "The damn fool! He must have been asleep!"

Dumarest snatched a bunch of flaming twigs from the fire and ran toward the hissing beast. It turned as he lashed at the eyes, mouth gaping to show gleaming fangs, ejecting a gust of noisome gas from its stomach. From above, the tip of its tail came whining down toward its tormentor. Dumarest jumped back as the barbs ripped his cloak.

"Watch it!" yelled Arn. "That damn tail can hit from any direction. "Lough!" he called again. "Bernie! What the hell are you waiting for!"

Shadows danced as they rushed in. Men scam-

pered: darting toward the beast, dodging the whip-
lash of the tail, stabbing with their spears and
smashing down with axes. The scaled hide was
tough and the beast quick on its clawed feet. It
turned, hissing; turned again as two men managed
to grab the tail while others smashed at the base of
its spine.

"Quick!" Arn was sweating, his scarred face
that of a demon. "Kill it before it can recover!
Before it can get free!"

More men grabbed the tail. Others beat at the
skull as it rose, bending backward so as to rip at the
men with its fangs, the amazingly flexible spine
permitting the creature to twist itself in any direction.

Dumarest plunged his spear into the exposed
throat. He ripped it free; struck again as the head
came down, blood gushing from the lacerated tissue. Fangs snapped at his leg, tore padding,
snapped again as Arn came rushing forward with a
great stone-bladed ax in his hands. He swung it,
using the full force of back and shoulder muscles.
The chipped edge of the stone bit into hide and
bone. He tore it loose and swung again, lips
thinned with desperation. His aim was good. The
blade hit where it had before and buried itself in
mass of blood and brain.

The zardle gave one convulsive twitch, then lay
still.

"The skull!" someone babbled. "Damn it, Arn,
you smashed the skull!"

Dumarest walked over to the guard as Arn dug
his fingers into the ruin of the skull. The man was

dead, his face lying in a pool of blood. He continued down the trail and reset the trip wire. Arn looked at him as he rejoined the hunter by the dead beast.

"Anything?"

"The guard's dead. I've reset the wire. Nothing else."

"Nothing here either," said Arn. He wiped his hands on the rags binding his legs. "The damn guard fell down on the job," he said. "Well, he deserved what he got. If it hadn't been for you the thing might have killed us all." He stood, brooding. "We'll strip him," he decided. "Share out what he's got. No sense in letting it go to waste."

"Nor this," said Dumarest. He kicked at the dead beast. "We can start a meal and have some left over. I'll get on with it while you attend to the dead man."

The heavy stone ax opened the carcass and hacked through the major joints. Knives finished the skinning, cut out the bones and internal organs. Men gathered snow and ice from the upper rocks, piled it into the skin together with chopped-up sections of tail, the soft brain, tongue and other organs. They lifted the primitive caldron to a support made of lashed spears hanging over a fire fed with fresh bone.

The flames rose, charred the skin, caused it to smoke and fuse on the outside, but could not burn through it—not while the water within kept the temperature below its flash point.

"By hell!" said a man later as he finished his stew. "Ain't nature wonderful? It provides meat, a cooking pot and fuel all in one piece.'' He reached out his bowl. ''Say, Bernie, any more of that tail left in there?''

''Sure,'' said Bernie.

''And tongue? I favor the tongue,'' said Lough.

''There's plenty for all,'' said Bernie. He smacked his lips. ''Man,'' he said with feeling. ''This is what I call real, honest-to-God eating!''

He grinned as he fished out a tender fragment of brain.

Two days later they came to a broken expanse of shattered rock and splintered stone ringing a scrub-covered declivity high in the mountains. A bowl scooped out among the soaring peaks and crags, sheltered from the winds and storm. A crust of snow clung to the dirt and scrub. Ice hung from the rocks above, looking like a cluster of threatening swords.

Dumarest crawled cautiously to the edge of the bowl and stared down. The sun was low on the horizon, the place full of shadows, and his breath plumed as he watched.

''Anything?'' Arn crawled up beside him, scarred face red and angry from the cold. He lifted a rag to cover his mouth and nose and block the vapor from his eyes. ''Could be anything down there,'' he mused. ''In among those shadows. Ten, twenty, even more. We wouldn't see them until they rushed us.''

''No,'' said Dumarest.

''One zardle's bad enough,'' said the hunter. ''Two is one too many. More is straight suicide.''

He squinted down into the declivity. "Let's hope your plan works."

The nets were of alloy mesh with a breaking strain of several tons, the mesh three inches square. Their normal use was to enmesh a beast while the hunters stabbed and hacked it to death. Sometimes the nets broke and more often the men let go, allowing a raging beast to wreak havoc among their numbers.

Dumarest had a different plan.

"We'll select a zardle," he said. "An old one. We'll snare it in the nets and then we'll leave it while we go after another. When we've caught as many as we've nets to hold, we'll go back to the first one. By then its struggles may have exhausted it. We'll open an artery and let it bleed to death."

"Simple," said Haran. He looked at Arn. "Why didn't you ever think of that?"

A scowl puckered the scar on the hunter's cheek. "How often have you seen a group of zardles?" he demanded. "And how often has anyone been able to supply more than a minimum number of nets? Of course I've thought of it," he stormed. "On Jec we used to hunt that way all the time. But the men knew how to take orders there. They weren't crazy to see blood, to search for a zerd." He looked at Dumarest. "How do we operate? In two parties?"

"You take Bernie, Lough and Wisar," said Dumarest. "I'll take the rest. Now remember, only go after a big one. Don't waste time on anything that's obviously young. Don't be sparing with the nets—I'd rather keep one than lose two.

And don't injure them," he added. "Don't spill any blood. I don't want the scent to frighten the others."

"You've hunted before," said Haran as they moved from the other group. "I never thought I'd see anyone who could tell Arn his business."

"I wasn't telling him," said Dumarest. "I was telling everyone. Reminding you all of what you may have forgotten. Now be quiet," he said to the group in general. "Don't talk and don't make any noise. Follow me and watch for my signals."

The scrub was thick in the bowl, the spined bushes growing higher than a man's head, intertwining so as to present an almost solid barrier at times. But paths wended through it where the beasts had forced a passage. Dumarest followed them, warily, checking when they came to a junction or emerged into an area of sparse growth.

He paused and listened. From the left came the soft rustle of the other party, sounding as if a wind rippled the tips of the bushes. From the right he could hear a regular medley of moving and tearing. He lifted his arm, pointed, stabbed twice with his finger, once to either side. Haran and one of the other men fanned out to cover the flanks. The fourth man stayed close behind Dumarest. He carried a spear while the rest held nets positioned, ready to throw.

Dumarest waited until everyone was in position, then stepped toward the grumbling noises. They grew louder as he approached, then suddenly fell silent. Stepping past a clump of scrub, Dumarest stared directly at a zardle.

The thing had been eating; the regular sound had been that of the mechanical champing of its jaws. It was big, fully thirty feet from nose to tip of vicious tail. The scaled hide had a peculiar dull sheen as of the patina on bronze.

Immediately it saw Dumarest: it attacked.

Dirt flew from beneath its clawed feet. The tail lashed up and over the spined head, slashing at the man before it. The mouth gaped, letting fall a fragment of thorned scrub, blasting a fetid odor.

Dumarest sprang to one side, hurled the net, snatched another as it fell over the head and tip of tail. He shook it out, poised and threw the glittering mesh. It sailed in a seemingly slow circle before settling almost on the other. Two more fell over the beast as Haran and the other man came running. Hissing, straining at the mesh, threshing with savage fury, the zardle was hopelessly trapped. Only the clawed feet and tip of the tail could move and then only for a few inches.

"All right," said Dumarest. "Let's get another."

The second was almost a repetition of the first and if anything was easier. They caught the beast from behind as it walked along one of the paths. A net thrown before it enmeshed its feet. A second entangled the back legs. Two others took care of head and tail.

Haran wiped his face, smiling. "Two," he gloated. "No trouble, no one lost, not even a scratch. Even if we don't find a zerd the trip hasn't been a waste." He looked to one side at the sound of a rustle. "That must be the others. We might as well join them."

Without nets there was nothing more they could do. Dumarest nodded. "We'll stay together from now on. Camp maybe and let the beasts lose their strength. Then we'll butcher and pack." He looked at the sky. "It'll be dark soon. We'd better hurry."

The rustle sounded again, faded away as they moved toward it. Dumarest took up the rear, Haran just ahead, the two other men before him. They broke into a run at the sound of shouts and yells. There was a hissing and a man screamed in pain.

"Wisar!" Haran lunged ahead, turned, snarling as Dumarest caught his cloak. "My brother! Let go, you—!" He tore free, lunged after the others, crashing through the scrub. Dumarest followed, protecting his face from the spines with uplifted arms. A second scream echoed as he burst into a clearing.

Before him stood nightmare.

It was big, vast—a creature from a prehistoric nightmare. The scaled hide was dull brown and green rippling on a fifty-foot frame, the head six feet above the ground. It hissed like a steam engine and the stench of its breath filled the air. Off to one side a smaller zardle lay struggling in a mesh of nets. Two men lay on the rocky soil—one broken, obviously dead, lying with his face in a pool of blood.

"Wisar!" Haran surged forward, struggled as

Dumarest gripped him, held him back. "Earl! That's my brother!"

"No, it isn't," snapped Dumarest. "Wisar wore a scarlet cloak in bands. That's in stripes. Bernie wore it."

Bernie, who had chuckled as he ate a zardle's brain.

"Where's Arn? Wisar?" Haran relaxed and Dumarest dropped his hands. "I can't see them anywhere. Can you? I—?" He broke off as the monstrous creature moved. "Down!"

Air whined as the tail lashed forward, hit a man, lifted him and threw him a broken bundle of rags into the clearing. His companion yelled and ran to where a spear lay on the ground.

"Come back, you fool!" Dumarest half-climbed to his feet, crouched, watching.

The man reached the spear, snatched it up and ran back toward the edge of the clearing. The rocky soil quivered as the monster lunged toward him. He twisted his head, screaming as the beast approached, tripping so that the spear flew from his hand as he hit the ground. Jaws gaped, closed, opened again to reveal red-stained teeth, red-stained rags.

"God!" Haran retched. "It bit him in half! Bit him right in half!"

Dumarest ducked as the tail swung again, cutting the spined scrub as a boy would lop a flower-head with a stick. "Arn!" he called. "Wisar!"

"Over here!" An arm waved from the circling scrub. "We got a zardle," shouted the hunter. "Netted it and were walking away when its mate arrived. Bernie and Lough got it right away. We managed to run and hide out in the scrub. I figured on meeting up with you so we could tackle it together. You got any nets?''

"No," yelled Haran. "Have you?"

"Some. Enough I think if we use them right. Do we get together?''

Dumarest lifted his head, shouted across the clearing. "No. If you try it and the thing attacks we wouldn't stand a chance. This way we can get at it from two directions. Get your nets ready. We'll distract it and you move in. Right?''

"When you're ready.''

"Now!" Dumarest rose, sprang forward and picked up the spear. He ran toward the beast, gesturing with the weapon, shouting. "Run to the right, Haran. Confuse it but watch for the tail. Now, Arn! What the hell are you waiting for?''

He heard the whine of air and sprang as the tail swept beneath him, whiplashed; jumped again as it swept back. A red eye glowed as the head turned. He aimed for it, flung the spear, grunted as the poorly balanced weapon glanced from a spined plate of horny armor. Again the tail lashed out. It hit the heel of his boot as he jumped, numbing his leg. Light glittered from the air as Wisar flung his net. It fell over the head, dropped to the ground. Another followed it, falling over the head, entangling one front leg. A third caught as the beast tried to charge. The force of its own effort sent it crashing to the ground.

"We've done it!" yelled Arn. "By God we've done it!''

He yelled again as the tip of the tail slammed against him, knocking him to the dirt, smashing the air from his lungs. Only the padding he wore saved him from being lacerated to the bone.

"More nets," said Dumarest. "Get more nets on the tail."

"We haven't got any," called Wisar. "We'll have to finish it off the hard way." He ran forward carrying an ax. "If I can just get one good chop at the spine—"

Dumarest ran forward and scooped up the spear. Again he dodged the tail and ran close to the head. The only way to finish the beast now was to puncture an artery and let it spill its life and strength on the ground. It had killed four men. That was more than enough.

He poised the spear and struck. The crude blade turned from the thick hide. He poised it again, gripped with both hands and drove it into the throat with the full energy of his body. A fountain of blood followed the spear as he tore it from the wound. He poised it for a second blow, then heard Haran's screamed warning.

"Earl! The tail! The tail!"

He jumped to one side and felt the barbs rip at his cloak. He looked as it rose, judged time and distance, jumped again as it swept down. Jumped—and felt his foot slip on the spilled blood, saw the sky and the thin whip of the tail, saw it lash toward his face.

Felt it strike with the brutal, stunning impact of a club.

Felt the savage barbs tear into the flesh of his eyes.

Somewhere a metronome was busy at work. *Tock! Tock! Tock! Tock! Tock! Tock!*

Dumarest relaxed, listening, wondering as to its rhythm. Too slow for a heartbeat, he decided, and too fast for minutes. An odd thing, he thought. One more odd thing to add to the rest. Why was he lying in bed between crisp sheets, for example. Why could he smell the unmistakable odor of a hospital? Why was he bandaged about the face? Why couldn't he see?

See?

Memory came rushing back on a thousand taloned feet.

He couldn't see because he was blind.

Blind!

BLIND!

He heard again the whispering voices as he swam up from darkness to a red-tinted hell of pain.

"Is he dead?" Wisar's voice, strained, worried.

"No, but it would be better if he was." Arn, coldly detached.

"I've heard you talk this way before." Haran, harshly gruff. "When Crin got hurt you wanted to leave him, pass him out easy. One day someone might do just that to you."

"They'd be doing me a favor. We'd be doing him one. Do you think he wants to sit around in the dark with a bowl, begging for his food? A man like Earl?"

A movement, the sharp hiss of indrawn breath, Haran's voice. "God! Look at his face! His eyes!"

"It's three days hard walking to get back to the village. We'd have to guide him every step of the way. More, we'd have to carry him, but that isn't the problem. He's been lashed with zardle poison. We haven't got an antidote. In a few hours he'll be going crazy with pain. In a week he'll be dead anyway. What's the point in letting him suffer?"

Wisar spoke from one side. "He deserves his chance. We owe him that for Crin. He helped when he didn't have to. You're with me in this, Haran. Our brother owes his life to this man. We can't forget that."

"But he's going to die anyway. . . . His woman might be able . . . leave it at that then . . . chance . . . try . . . owe it to him."

A mounting cacophony of blurred and meaningless voices drowned out by the pain of his lacerated eyes, the pain of his mental awareness, the searing agony of the nerve poison already at work.

And then nothing but pain, pain, pain and screaming agony going on and on and on. . . .

Dumarest stiffened, nails digging into his palms, forcing himself to be calm. That pain and madness belonged to the past. It was over now. Done with. Only one thing remained.

He was blind.

Blind and stranded.

The blindness in itself was nothing. Eyes could be repaired or replaced, but not without money. And he had no money, and without eyes, no hope of getting any.

Blind!

He heard the opening of a door, the scuff of feet, the blurred sounds of voices. Someone stood beside him and he felt the touch of cold metal. A snipping sound as scissors cut away the bandage. A glow of brightness, a sudden flood of light.

He could see! See!

"A first-class job." The doctor wore green and sported a small beard. Light flashed from an instrument in his hand. He clucked in self-satisfaction. "Perfect! As good a pair of eyes as anyone could wish." He snapped off the light, straightened, put away the instrument. "You're a lucky man," he said to Dumarest. "In more ways than one. The blow wasn't serious as it might have been; apparently you blocked most of it with a spear you were carrying. The eyes were ruined, true, but not so badly that we didn't have all the tissue we needed to grow replacements. You must have incredible fortitude and you have good friends. They carried you lashed in a zardle skin, your hands bound so that you couldn't tear out your eyes. The pain you must have suffered—" He shrugged. "I don't suppose you want to remember that. But your eyes are all right now. You are as fit as we can make you. And," he ended, "you have a visitor. I guess you want to see her alone."

She had reclaimed the golden tunic and wore it with a proud defiance, aware of her beauty and aware of what the golden fabric did for it. Her hair was a blazing mass of rippling fire. Emeralds shone in her eyes.

"Earl!"

She was warm and soft and wonderful against the bare flesh of his arms and torso. Perfume wafted from her hair, accentuated her femininity. Around his body her arms were like steel.

"Darling! I was worried," she said. "So worried. But everything's all right now."

"Tell me."

"They brought you back, Arn and the two brothers. They made a pact with each other. If they found nothing they would have killed you. Given you a merciful ending. But they found zerds. Enough to pay for Crin's operation, to buy you new eyes, to buy High passage for all of us. We're safe now, darling. Safe!"

He sat up in the bed. He felt fit, healed, ready for anything. Slow-time therapy had compressed two days of healing into a single hour of sleep. The companion drug to quick-time which had the opposite effect. He swung long legs from the bed and caught the glitter of movement at the corner of his eyes. He turned, facing the sink, the dripping faucet which was his fancied metronome.

He looked at the woman, wonderful with visual impact, warm and human with the promise of life.

"Kalin," he said. "You are so very beautiful."

Her eyes flickered, straightened. "Get dressed, Earl. Our ship is leaving soon."

"You've booked passage? To where?"

"To Solis, darling," she said. "To home."

XII

SHADOWS FILLED THE room: thick, clustering, broken only by the steady green eye of the signal light, the pale intrusion of the day outside. Mede's voice was a hypnotic modulation, relentlessly repetitive, a sonic drill to penetrate the fog of disoriented senses.

"Where is Brasque? Tell me where to find your husband! Where is he hiding? Tell me where to find Brasque! Where is your husband? Where is your husband? Where is your husband?"

Not in the house, not on the land around the house, not anywhere on the planet as far as the cyber could determine. And yet, logically, this was the place to which he would have run. To his planet, his home, his wife and friends. The prediction had a probability of ninety-nine percent, which made it a practical certainty.

He had to be found!

Mede turned from the woman, accepting temporary defeat. His voice was not enough but there were other ways. Instruments could smash through the coma and detachment, force a way to the receptive areas of the brain, reward cooperation and punish stubbornness. And, if the questioning killed her, it didn't matter, providing he gained what he wanted. What the Cyclan wanted and must obtain at any cost.

Mede left the room, passed through the antechamber and nodded to the girl waiting outside in the open place facing the sea. "You may return to your place now."

She dipped a curtsy, not quite knowing how to treat the enigmatic figure in flaming scarlet. He had the freedom of the house and access to her charge at all times and this by the direct order of the Master himself. And yet, despite his attention, the Lady Keelan showed no signs of improvement.

She scuttled away as the cyber walked to the edge of the patio and stared down at the rocks and swirling water below. The sea was rough with winter memory, the waves savage as they boomed against the foot of the cliff, spume flying as they frothed about the stone. A faint wind carried the scent of brine and open spaces, teasing the edge of his cowl, so that at one minute it ballooned and the next was pressed hard against the bone structure of his face.

He turned as Komis walked toward him across the open space. The Master of Klieg looked tired, haggard from a growing sense of the inevitable. It had been a long, hard winter.

His eyes flickered to the closed door of the antechamber. "Any improvement?"

"None, my lord."

"It's been a long time," said Komis. "All winter, to be exact. I had hopes that perhaps you—" He broke off, shaking his head. "I hoped for too much," he admitted. "How could you succeed where physicians fail?"

"The Cyclan has methods of its own, my lord," said Mede smoothly. "I have tried verbal stimulation and hypnotic techniques but they are not enough. The stimulus must be stronger. With your permission, my lord, I would like to try certain devices much used on worlds dedicated to mental care."

Komis hesitated. "Instruments?"

"Sensory stimulators, my lord. Have I your permission?"

"No," said Komis; yet where was the harm? "I must think about it," he temporized. "I do not wish my sister to be the subject of experiments. Leave it for now."

Mede bowed. "As you wish, my lord. In the meantime I have been working on certain problems regarding matters we have spoken of earlier. The question of diverting land and labor to other uses than the rearing of horses. The predictions are highly favorable and—"

"Later, cyber." Komis felt a sudden relief. If the man had really worked out a system by which they could gain wealth, then his worries were over. Money to expand, to build, to provide what Keelan must have. "We will discuss it after dinner," he said. "Now I intend to relieve Mandris so that she can attend church."

"Church, my lord?"

"Yes. Some monks of the Brotherhood are here with a portable church. They come several times a year and ease the souls of those who have sinned." He smiled a little as he thought of the girl. "Mandris is not what I would call a sinful girl but it will do her no harm to bend her knee and eat the bread of forgiveness."

Dumarest stretched, filling his lungs with the scented air of spring, glancing at the green of rolling hills. The landing field was small but large enough for a planet with little trade. It was well-tended, the crushed gravel clean and without unwanted growth. Beyond the fence lay the town, a place of long, low buildings made of logs and stone, a few of concrete, still less of mortared brick. Pens stood to one side, warehouses the other.

"A nice planet," he said to Kalin. "It should grow nice people."

She smiled and led him through the gate. A man stepped forward as they approached. He was big, dressed in rough weave from a hand-operated loom and his hair was as red as the girl's.

"Transport, sir?" Green eyes swept over them as he touched one finger to his forehead.

Dumarest looked at Kalin. "Do we need it? How far must we go?"

"Too far to walk. The house of Klieg," she said to the driver. You know it?"

"A long flight, my lady."

"I did not ask that. Do you know where it is?"

He bowed. "I know, my lady. You wish to be taken to the house?"

"A moment. Is there a public communicator close to hand?"

A booth stood at the edge of the field close to the gate. Dumarest waited as she made her call. She was in the booth for a long time, and when she came out, she was solemn. Silently she climbed into the cabin of the waiting flier. Dumarest followed her and the driver locked them in.

"The thren are most dangerous at this time of year," he explained as he took his seat. "The canopy is proof against their attacks, but if you should forget, open it a little—" He shrugged. "Their beaks are long," he said. "The risk not worth taking."

Dumarest settled back as the flier climbed into the sky.

"Earl!"

He looked at his arm, the fingers digging into his flesh; the wide, frightened eyes. Gently he eased her fingers. "You're doing it again," he accused. "Why? What good does it do to know just what is going to happen?"

"If you knew," she said, "would you refuse to look?"

"No," he admitted. "Probably not. But, to me, the future is what I make it. I can win or I can lose, but I will always try." He smiled and dropped his arm about her shoulders. "Be cheerful," he urged. "You're almost home."

"We're almost home," she corrected. "I hope you like the house of Klieg. It is big and warm and comfortable. Strong too. When the winds really blow you can feel the walls fighting back and when the snow falls the roof seems to shrug as it accepts the burden. It's a nice house, Earl. A wonderful house."

His arm tightened around her shoulders. "It isn't the place that's important. It's who you are with."

She smiled and traced a pattern on the back of his hand with the tip of a finger. "Earl, how important is physical beauty to you? I mean, if a woman was old or ugly, could you love her? Really love her?"

"I don't have to," he said. "Not while I have you."

"Please, Earl! I'm serious!"

"And so am I." He turned so as to stare into her face, meet the emerald of her eyes. "You are you," he said slowly. "If you were to have an accident, lose your beauty in some way, it would make no difference to the way I feel. I didn't fall in love with a pair of green eyes, some white skin and red hair. I fell in love with a woman."

Her hand gripped his, tightened. "Earl. What would you say if I told you—" She broke off.

Dumarest frowned. "You're trying to tell me something," he said. "Something important. Is it to do with the future?"

"I know what is going to happen," she said

dully. "But that isn't important. Earl, what would you say if I told you that I'd lied? That my real name isn't Kalin? That—"

She fell silent as he rested his fingers on her lips. "Listen," he said. "The past is dead. Forget it."

"But—"

"There are no 'buts,' " he interrupted. "Don't tell me something you may later regret. Something I may not want to hear. I don't care what happened before I met you. As far as I'm concerned your past doesn't exist. I simply want you now, as you are, for always."

"Thank you, Earl," she said quietly. "I wish—God how I wish that!"

"Please." He lifted his hand and touched her cheek. It was wet with tears. "Please, darling, don't upset yourself. Don't do that."

"Earl," she said. "I love you. I love you, but I know I'm going to lose you. I—"

The flier banked, began to drop in a wide turn. The driver spoke without turning his head. "Klieg, my lady. Directly below."

Komis met them, helping the girl from the cabin, paying the driver, examining Dumarest with a single glance of his eyes. Green eyes like those of the girl, the driver, everyone else on the planet who had been reared from the pure strain. Eyes and hair and translucent skin. Peas from the same genetic pod.

"You are welcome," said Komis and extended his hand. "May Klieg protect you during your stay."

Dumarest gripped the proffered hand. "As I shall protect Klieg should the need arise."

Komis widened his eyes in pleasure at the unexpected response. "You accept your obligations," he said. "I had not thought you to be aware of our customs."

"I'm not," said Dumarest evenly. "But I have stayed in similar houses before." Stayed and fought when the need arose, and though here there was no need, the implication remained. A guest should be willing to aid those who gave him hospitality.

"I'll have someone show you to your room," said Komis. "You probably wish to bathe and rest before the evening meal." He turned to the girl. "And now, my dear, we have much to discuss. I am sure that your friend will excuse us."

She turned to Dumarest. "Earl. I—"

"You have to go," he interrupted. "I understand. But remember that you don't have to worry. Not about anything." He smiled and kissed her and watched as she followed the Master of Klieg. Gold and white and flaming red. Bright and wonderful against the wood and stone of the house, the gray cobbles set in the ground of the yard. Then she vanished through a door and he turned to follow his guide.

The water was hot, the soap plentiful, the bathroom a place of planked walls and plastic fittings with unguents and lotions in crystal jars. Dumarest bathed, sponged down his clothing and went to examine the house. To the landward side the yard held the hint of a stable-smell. Closer he caught the scent of baking bread, of smoke and leather and stored grain. Inside the dwelling he paused in the hall and examined the weapons hanging under the great beams of the roof. Spears and bows, axes and partisans, cross-hilted swords and curved daggers. Over the fireplace someone had set the crossed bills of dead threns. The table was marked and gouged with egotism and time, the wood glowing with wax, the names and insignia shadows flickering in the fading light of day.

Home, he thought, Kalin was born here, ran through this very hall, perhaps, playing with her toys. Home.

He turned and saw a dusty flame of scarlet, the pale face beneath the shadowing cowl. Light caught the seal emblazoned on the breast and turned it to glittering brilliance.

Mede saw Dumarest and paused, watching. Dumarest frowned. A cyber? Here?

Such men were usually to be found at the heart of things, the courts and centers of business where their influence would be the greatest, their services in most demand. Klieg was nothing more than a fortified manor. An overgrown farmhouse fitted with modern devices and housing a family together with servants and retainers. There was nothing really important or grand about the place. Certainly they couldn't afford the services of a cyber to advise them as to which crops to plant, what to sell and when.

Dumarest stepped close to Mede, feeling his nerves tense, his hatred for the man and what he stood for rise in a surging wash of red. The Cyclan had cost him too much for him to easily forget.

"An unusual place to find you, cyber," he said, masking his feelings. "Is there much to interest you on Solis?"

"All things are of interest, my lord." Mede was smooth, politely emotionless as his eyes searched Dumarest's face. "Are you a member of this house?"

"A guest." Dumarest was curt. The hall was no longer a place of comfort and imagining. The cyber had contaminated it by his presence. He walked past the immobile figure in the scarlet robe and down a short passage. It led to Komis' study. The door opened and Kalin stepped through.

"Earl!"

"Is something wrong?" She looked distraught. "Kalin. Tell me."

"Nothing is wrong." Komis stood behind her, his eyes incredulous. "She is unharmed and will continue to be so. There will be no punishment for her desertion."

"Punishment?" Dumarest stepped forward and faced the other man. "There will be no punishment," he said softly. "You are correct in that. It would not be wise to hurt the girl in any way."

"Please, Earl!" She stepped before him, small hands hard against his chest. "You don't understand. There's no need to threaten. Komis wouldn't hurt me."

"I do not think your friend was making threats," said the Master of Klieg. "I took it more in the nature of a prophecy. But she is right," he said to Dumarest. "You do not understand. You couldn't. Even I still have doubt and—'' He broke off, looking baffled. "A man must believe the evidence of his senses. There is no way this girl could have known of the things she told me unless what she claims is true. Therefore I must believe her. Believe what she claims.''

Dumarest was curt. "And that is?''

"That her name is Mallini Frenchi of Sard. That she came here five years ago, running away from her home and family to take up service with my house. That two years ago she deserted her post.''

"Is that all?" Dumarest smiled. "A name," he said. "What is in a name?''

"Please, Earl," she whispered. "There is more.''

"I don't want to hear it.''

Komis stepped forward, face hard beneath the white skin, lips thinned so that he looked suddenly hard and cruel. "You must," he repeated. "Because this affects the house, the family of Klieg. The girl is not what you think. Her body is that of Mallini Frenchi but not her mind. That belongs to my sister, the Lady Keelan of Klieg. My sister who has not left her bed for more than seven years!''

XIII

DIMNESS WHICH BLURRED outline, a suspicion of a shape lying in the suspicion of a bed. Pipes and metering devices and a single green lamp which shone like a living emerald and told that life still lasted, the heart still beat, the body still functioned.

After a fashion, of course. In its own, peculiar way.

"Earl!"

The voice was a rasping whisper without depth or emotion, a strained vibration which hung on the air like the gossamer web of a spider, light and frail, a quiver among the shadows, a ghost voice whispering ghost words.

Dumarest leaned forward, eyes narrowed as he tried to penetrate the dark. "Yes?"

"Earl! Please! They told you. I told you. You know that I am Kalin. The girl you said you loved."

He hesitated. The girl was outside with Komis sitting on the stone bench facing the sea.

"Remember Logis? Remember how we fled the ship and drifted in the sac? Remember how you bought our freedom from the slaver and how, for three days, we tasted Heaven. Three days and more. Earl. Much more. My darling, my dearest, my beloved! I love you. I love you. God help me, I love you!"

A rail stood at the foot of the shadowed bed. Dumarest grasped it and felt the sweat bead his forehead as the ghost voice, rasping, horrible, stirred the air with things only Kalin could possibly know. Intimate things. Words and deeds which had sealed one to the other. He remembered the look of incredulity on Komis' face, the stunned acceptance of belief.

"Seven years ago I was the beauty of Solis," whispered the voice. "I married a brilliant man. Brasque was a biochemist and life-technician, the best on Solis. On our honeymoon in the Soaring Hills our camp was attacked by some thren. We beat them off but in the flurry I was scratched. A minor wound, we thought, nothing to worry about. But a week later my arm began to swell. In another five days I couldn't walk. I have never walked since."

"An infection," said Dumarest. "But surely anitibiotics would have cured such a thing?"

"Do you think Brasque didn't try? The disease

was unique. A relatively minor infection was
caused by bacteria carried by the thren. So much
we discovered. But, here on Solis, we are the
victims of ancestors who held a paranoid's dream.
Red hair was a sign of superiority, they claimed.
And so they bred for the true color. Bred and
inbred and inbred until we developed unsuspected
weaknesses. The infection, harmless to you, to
the majority on this planet, triggered off a terrible reaction. I say 'terrible,' because to me,
that is what it was. I became—different. More
than that. I became a thing of horror, a burden, a
disgusting . . . "

"Stop it!"Dumarest's hands clamped on the rail
as he leaned forward. "Stop it!"

A wet slobbering, a shifting, a waft of repellent
odor. A mechanism clicked as it fed a tran-
quilizing solution into the blood. Another metered
sedative. The rasping whisper blurred a little.

"Brasque came back. Helped me. And, Earl,
suddenly I was fit again. I could walk and talk and
dance! I could see desire in the eyes of men. I
could travel and taste the delights of the galaxy.
What did it matter if I starved or begged or traveled
Low? I was alive and free and every single second
was paradise." The voice choked in a liquid gur-
gling. "Can you guess, my darling, how I felt? Can
you ever guess?"

Sitting blinded as men discussed his fate. Traveling in a hell of pain. Wondering what life had to
offer and then, miraculously, he could see again!

"Yes," said Dumarest tightly. "I can guess how
you felt."

"And love," she said. "Real love. Warm love. Your love, my dearest. You remember what you said? That it wouldn't matter how I looked, you would still love me? You remember that?"

"I remember."

"Then turn on the light," whispered the rasping gurgle. "Turn on the light—and see the real me."

Triggered by the sonic command the room began to brighten with a pearly luster. Plates glowed in roof and walls, truglow plates which showed things as they really were, devoid of artifice and optical trickery. Dumarest looked at the thing on the bed.

There was a head, bald, shining, creased like a mass of crumpled crepe, swollen to twice normal size. The eyes were thin glittering slits, the mouth a lipless gash and the chin was a part of the composite whole which was the neck.

A sheet covered the body with its strange and alien protuberances. Pipes ran from beneath it and connected to quietly humming machines. Tanks and instruments completed the life-support installation.

"Nice, isn't it?" The lips didn't move as the voice drifted weakly past them. "A metabolism run wild. Carcinoma barely controlled by extensive surgery and continuous medication. Seven years, Earl. Five of them utter hell."

The metal of the rail bent beneath his hands. "Kalin!"

"Yes, Earl, the woman you swore you loved. Not the eyes and skin and mane of hair but the real woman. The mind and soul and personality. The things which loved you, Earl, those things are here. The rest is a pretty shell. Which did you love, Earl? The brain or the body? Me or that beautiful shell? Which, Earl? Which?''

He took a deep breath, remembering. This woman had saved his life, given back his eyes, given him her love. He released the rail and stepped toward the head of the bed.

''Kalin,'' he said. ''I shall always love you.''

And kissed the slitted lips.

''You were kind,'' said Komis. ''I shall always remember that.''

Dumarest stared at the stone, the beams, the hanging weapons. Firelight threw shadows across his face. Komis reached out and poured wine, pushed a goblet across the table.

''Drink,'' he ordered. ''I know how you must feel. When the girl told me who she really was it was as if the world had turned upside down.'' He drank, setting an example. ''They are together now.''

Dumarest emptied his goblet. ''Why?'' he demanded.

''They are talking, doing something, I don't know what.''

''I don't mean why are they together. But why tell me? Why make me see Kalin as she really is?''

Komis poured more wine. ''Keelan,'' he said. ''Her name is Keelan.''

''Keelan, Kalin, they are like enough.'' To Dumarest the wine was like water. ''She wanted to prove something,'' he said. ''Wanted to know if I loved her or a pretty face. But I love the whole woman. Not an empty shell. Not a diseased woman lying helpless on a bed. I want someone who—''

''I know what you want, Earl.'' She came forward as they rose, smiling, a large ring weighing one finger. ''I am whole again,'' she said. ''As I was when we made love on the slaver's ship, gambled in Pete's Bar on Chron. Your woman, Earl. Not half but complete again—for now and perhaps for always.''

Komis frowned. ''You speak in riddles, sister. There is much I do not understand.''

''You will,'' she promised. ''And now, brother, if you will excuse us? I must talk with Earl alone.'' She sat as he left and helped herself to wine. Teeth gleamed as she lifted the goblet and her eyes held a sparkling green fire. ''To love, Earl,'' she said. ''To love and to us!''

The goblets made empty rapping sounds on the table.

''I was unfair, Earl, to make you prove your love for me the way I did. But the ego is a peculiar thing. Always it must be reassured and rejection is tantamount to death.'' She looked at the ring on her finger. ''Death,'' she repeated, and shuddered.

Silently he poured them both more wine.

''Brasque was an unusual man,'' she said. ''Clever, intelligent, dedicated. When it became obvious that I would never be well again he left Solis. For years I heard nothing and then, one night, he returned. It was a time of storm. The air was full of sleet and it was very late. No one saw him but my attendant and myself. And he was dying, Earl. Dying.''

She took a sip of wine. ''All the time he'd been away he'd been searching for some means to help me. Incredibly he found it. Somehow he'd managed to get himself employed on a special project in an unusual laboratory which dealt in the life-sciences. Not too difficult, really, for he was very clever. He found what he was looking for. He called it an affinity-twin. A life-form based on a molecular chain of fifteen units and the reversal of one unit would make it either dominant or subject. He stole it, Earl. I think he killed to get it. I know that he thought he was being followed.

''He was wounded, terribly, his body filled with poisons, but he would not stop until he had done what he had come to do. The life-form was an artificially created symbiote. It nestles in the rear of the cortex, meshes with the thalmus and takes control of the central nervous system. So Brasque told me, Earl. But he was dying and there was little time for explanations. He injected something into my skull—something into the skull of my attendant. I felt dizzy for a moment and then, suddenly, I was Mallini.

''Can you imagine it, Earl? After years as a diseased and decaying woman I was suddenly alive again. Young and beautiful and wonderfully active. In another person's body, true, but what did that matter? It felt like my body. It was my body. I could walk and dance and lift my head to look at the sky. Life, Earl! Life!''

He sat, thinking, looking at his goblet of wine.

"This girl whose body you took over," he said quietly. "What happened to her?"

"Mallini?" She shrugged. "I don't know. Brasque wasn't sure or didn't tell me. I think that her mind became a part of my own, that we shared all the things I did and enjoyed doing." Her hand reached out and touched his. "Enjoyed doing so very much, Earl. So very, very much."

Dumarest remained serious. "And if she . . . you . . . her . . . should die, what then?"

"I don't know," she said. "Earl, that is what frightens me. I look ahead and things are confused. I—the me that you see lives, but is it really me? The body lives but am I in it? I want to be in it. I think that if it were done carefully I would stay as I am even though that diseased thing upstairs should die—cease functioning. I want to be free of it, Earl. Wholly free. Sometimes, as if in a dream, I come back and . . . and. . ."

Her face changed, contorted. "Earl!"

"Kalin! What is it?"

"No!" Her mouth opened, breath rasping in her throat. "No I won't come back. No! No! No! Stop it!" she screamed. "Earl! Help me!"

And, suddenly, her face went blank. The eyes were still green, still open but they were empty as the windows of a deserted house. The lips moved, still red, still soft, but the smile was the loose grimace of an idiot.

"Kalin!"

Dumarest sprang to his feet, ran down the passage, up the stairs, through the room and out onto the patio where sea-sound filled the air and sea-scent blew through the pillars.

The door to the antechamber was open. He ran through it and into the place of shadows. The shadows had gone, dissolved in a flood of light from the truglow tubes. Metal and crystal sparkled from the life-support apparatus. At the head of the bed the scarlet robe of the cyber glowed like fresh-spilled blood.

"No!" The voice from the creature on the bed was a pain-filled gasp of protest. "No!"

"Where is your husband?" Mede's voice held no hate, no urgency, but the level monotone was all the more inhuman because of that. A hum came from something in his hands. "Where is your husband?"

"He's dead!" The croak was more terrible than a scream. "Dead! Dead! Dead!" And then, horribly, "Earl, my darling! Earl!"

The signal lamp changed from green to red.

Dumarest sprang forward as the cyber rose. He saw the movement of the hand from the wide sleeve, the flash, felt the burn. He gripped the wrist as Mede fired again, the laser searing plastic and metal and flesh before it fell from the broken hand.

"You killed her! Tortured her to death!"

Mede stabbed the fingers of his left hand toward Dumarest's eyes. He fought with a cold detachment as he jerked his knee toward the groin, swung his elbow toward the face. Dumarest blocked the attack, struck once and gripped the robe as Mede sagged. Strength blossomed from his fury. This man had killed Kalin! This thing had again robbed him of happiness!

He heaved the scarlet figure into the air, ran from the room to the patio, to where the pillars looked down onto the sea and rocks below. For a moment he stood poised, the weight of the cyber struggling in his hands, then he stepped forward and threw the scarlet figure over the edge.

And watched as the sea cleaned the red of blood and fabric from the granite teeth studding the shore.

Brother Jerome folded his hands within the sleeves of his robe and glanced at the shining majesty of Arsini's statue. "Tell me," he said to Dumarest. "Do you also believe that all men originated on one small world?"

Dumarest remained silent. He was thinking of a girl and the long journey to Hope and in him the sense of loss was an aching wound. Kalin was dead. The cyber had killed her with his questioning, but the body he remembered still lived. It was as lovely, the skin as white, the hair as red as before, but something had gone from the eyes. Kalin had loved him but Mallini did not and he could find nothing to love in Mallini. The package was the same but the contents were not.

"Brasque, of course, must have worked in one of the laboratories somehow connected with the Cyclan," said the Head Monk, casually. He smiled at Dumarest's expression. "We know about it," he explained. "More, perhaps, than you guess. The ring you are wearing, for example. Komis gave it to you. It was the last gift Brasque gave his wife and she wanted you to have it in case something happened as, of course, she knew it would.''

"She knew but she could do nothing about it," said Dumarest tiredly. "She didn't even try."

"Some things cannot be avoided," said Brother Jerome quietly. "Call it fate if you wish. And her ability was strange to her. A side-effect of the symbiote she carried in her brain." He led the way down a winding path. "That is what Mede was after. Brasque must have stolen the secret and been wounded making his escape. He landed at Klieg on a stormy night. He did what he had to do and then, to hide his trail, threw himself from the patio into the sea. The woman, call her Kalin, took his flier and began her travels. As far as Komis was concerned the girl had simply deserted.

"But the Cyclan wanted what Brasque had stolen. They sent men to search and Mede was the one who found the logical place. But he did not know that Brasque was dead."

Dumarest kicked at a stone. "If they developed it, then why couldn't they repeat it? The Cyclan do not lack for experts."

"I think it had to do with luck," said the High Monk carefully. "Or, perhaps, the workings of destiny. I think it safe to assume that Brasque stumbled on the correct sequence by chance. Fifteen units on a molecular chain. Even if you knew which units to work with, can you guess how long it would take to cover every possible combination? Over four thousand years," he said. "That is trying one new combination each second. How much longer would it take if each combination required a day? No, brother, the cyber was desperate to learn where Brasque could be found. The Cyclan does not like failure."

Dumarest looked at the ring on his finger. A flat, polished stone set in a heavy band of gold. It was a man's ring; on Kalin it had looked enormous.

"And the girl?" he asked. "What happens to her?"

"She will stay here until her father comes to take her back to Sard," said Jerome. "I was wrong about that man," he admitted. "Centon Frenchi is just what he claims to be. Now, perhaps, he can bring himself to love his daughter."

"Is that so hard?"

"It is when you are proud and your daughter is an atavist. The coloring was bad enough but she was more. A little simple," said the monk softly. "Easily hurt and easily frightened. Unwanted by the others of her family. She ran away, to the planet from which her grandmother had originated, and there she took service with the Master of Klieg."

Dumarest followed the monk down the path and along a diverging track. "How is she? I mean, does she remember very much of what happened?"

"No. To her it is all a vague dream. The symbiote was extremely effective." He halted before a flowering shrub. "Can you imagine the power of a thing like that? Not immortality but something so attractive to the old, the crippled, the diseased that they would pay anything to obtain it. A new body. Literally new. A body to use and abuse, to kill with and be killed in. Something which would give a true proxy life. A thing which—" He broke off. "Fifteen units," he said after a moment. "I pray that they may never again be united in a correct sequence. That the secret died with the man who stole it."

He took a deep breath, savoring the scent of the flowers. "We grow morbid, brother. A bad emotion for such a day. You have plans?"

"To travel," mused Dumarest. "To travel. What else?"

"To travel," mused Jerome. "To search. To look for something you may never find." He looked at the hard face, the eyes with their fading scars. Dedication sometimes took strange forms. "You are welcome to stay as my guest for as long as you wish. I would advise, however, that you do not see the girl again. A man should not torment himself," he explained gently. "She is not as you remember her."

"I know," said Dumarest. Would he ever find someone like Kalin again?

"I will instruct Brother Fran to give you a warrant for a High passage on any ship leaving this planet," continued the High Monk. "You may use it when you wish. And there is more," he added. "Centon Frenchi has been most generous. You will not leave as a pauper."

"Thank you, Brother," said Dumarest. "You are gracious."

The High Monk bowed and walked away.

Alone, Dumarest wandered the gardens before sitting on a bench. There were things to do, plans to make. Here, on Hope, were records which could be of interest. The archives of the Church of the Universal Brotherhood would contain, perhaps, the coordinates of Earth. Forgotten, discarded, a fragment in the mass of information.

He sat, hands beside him, the stone of the ring on his finger glowing in the light of the sun.

Glowing brighter as the statue began to sing. Shining as the sonic impulse triggered the buried "memory" of the lustrous material. Dumarest didn't see it. He concentrated on the statue, the impressive figure straining up and away from the flaming orb. On his finger the glow concentrated into fifteen spots of brilliance, each descriptive of a molecular unit.

Brasque's secret.

Unnoticed in Dumarest's dream of Earth.